KING OF
Fury

KING OF FURY, Vows of Blood, Book 2

© 2026 by Willow York

Cover Art by Wicked Smart Designs

Editor Grace Bradley Editing, LLC

ISBN: 978-1-7644575-1-4

NOTE:

Trigger Warning: This story includes scenes depicting sexual assault.

ONE

DALLEN

I SEE HIM BEFORE HE SEES ME. THE GUY RADIATES hot, rough sex—exactly what I need tonight. I want to forget who I am and the overly involved family I come from. At twenty-eight, I'm more than ready to make my own choices, and tonight I'm making a big one.

One that I've never made before.

Would he go for it if I talked to him? I shivered at the idea of boldness. At work, I'm confident, capable, and sharp—but in a nightclub, squeezed into a tight dress and too much makeup (though my bestie claimed it looked natural), I feel lost and anxious.

Damn it, I can't do it.

Yes, you can, Dallen!

I squirm and sip my vodka and orange. It's not trendy, but I like it—nothing too strong, tastes like juice. I need Dutch courage. I'm usually cautious, maybe thanks to my upbringing, but tonight will be different.

I could do this. I could.

A bass pulse thuds through the floor beneath my heels, the kind of beat that makes the whole room vibrate in waves.

"What about him?" I grab hold of my best friend Amy's arm and nod toward where the god stands beside the dance floor, his eyes skimming the nightclub like a bouncer, not so much a patron. He looks so out of place, like his attire alone says businessman, and yet I'm pretty sure I see a few tattoos poking out of his white, unbuttoned shirt and on his hands. When he shifts, and the light catches his chest.

I sigh, wanting him more than I should. I'm probably setting myself up for disappointment. He may be here with someone—his girlfriend, or boyfriend, or both. Who the fuck knows? But I won't let the unknowns get me down. Since I still don't know, that means I have a chance.

And I want him to be my first. It's high time I lose my V-card, and he looks like he knows what to do with a woman.

"Oh fuck yes, he's hot. Damn," Amy whines, pulling herself up on the stool beside me. "I'm depressed now that you saw him first. He's so fucking hot." She gasps and clasps my arm. "Unless you want to share him?"

I laugh and push Amy off. "Not my vibe, but thanks. I'm flattered." I glance back at the god, now talking to a brunette, hope fading. He laughs at something she says, and I stare—he's so pretty.

Pretty and mysterious at the same time.

"Looks like he's taken."

"Yeah." I turn away, looking for the bartender. I need a stronger drink. Even if I hate liquor, I need a hit after that blow.

Amy chuckles and wraps her arm about my shoulder. "Cheer up, there will be others. We have to get you to lose your virginity tonight if it's the last thing we do. While I think the guy was hot as fuck and probably knew how to make a woman come just by looking at her, he may have been a little advanced in the sexual department than what we want for you tonight...if you know what I mean."

"You mean you think I should be able to walk normally tomorrow, and that guy's undoubtedly large, capable cock wouldn't allow that."

A coughing sound to my side makes me aware our conversation—even in the thrumming, loud music of the nightclub—isn't as private as I'd hoped. I turn and feel the blood run from my body. In fact, I'm pretty sure I die in my chair.

The god of a man that had been chatting up the pretty brunette is beside me, his wicked, amused smirk sending my heart into overdrive. I thought he was fucking hot from half a room away, but now, up close— damn it all to fucking Hades—this guy is gorgeous.

And tattooed, just as I thought. My eyes dip to his strong jaw, his wicked mouth that's grinning at me. He does have tatts on his chest, but I can't make out what they're about; they're dark and not colored. He's tanned, dark-haired, looks like he's stepped off the Mediterranean beach, and yet here he is in a nightclub in New York.

Next to me.

Smirking.

"Hey."

Holy shit, he's talking to me. I force myself to stay calm, resisting the urge to freeze like a deer in head-lights. I manage a hesitant smile, feeling exposed standing next to him now that he's heard. "I guess you heard what I said."

He chuckles. The sound is deep, cultured, and— holy shit—Amy has joked about getting wet over guys. I've always thought she was on crack. But here I am, eating humble pie. My panties are wet—all thanks to one guy in this club, now speaking to me.

"The part about the large cock making tomorrow tough?" He smiles like before, and I fight not to swoon.

"Yeah, I heard. I hope that doesn't happen—unless you meant me. Then I'm open to negotiations."

WHATTTTTTTT.

I hear Amy squeal into her drink behind me, but thankfully she doesn't interrupt. For a moment, I don't know what to say. I've never been in this position before. I've never had a guy I've wanted in my bed hint at joining me there as well.

"What about your girlfriend?"

He looks puzzled before he leans on one elbow, studying me. "I don't have a girlfriend."

"But I saw you talking to a woman just before."

"That's my brother's fiancée. She's not mine."

She's not mine?

Wow, was that how he spoke about the women he dated? Like they were his property—something for him to protect? To own. To lay claim to. Shit, that was hot, and not something I thought I'd be into, but...here we are.

"What would our negotiations consist of if we were to discuss that particular partnership later tonight?" I say.

He rubs his jaw, as if weighing my reckless proposal. He can't be. I can feel my pulse hammering at the thought of being so bold—so unlike myself. But tonight I've sworn I'm done haunting the city as the lonely, desperate twenty-eight-year-old virgin.

I want to lose my V-card. I need to live and explore. This guy seems like the perfect place to start.

Somewhere behind us, glassware clinks sharply at the bar, noise slicing through the music like a reminder of how real this moment suddenly is.

Near the dance floor, colored lights flicker over the crowd, casting brief flashes across his face that make his expression look even more dangerous and unreadable.

"What do you want me to do?" he says, and I'm dead.

Again.

TWO

STEPHEN

How can I refuse a lady's offer? I stare down at the pretty little redhead—Pumpkin, I decide to call her. Even in the middle of July, she looks like a woman who suits fall.

I bet she wears those ridiculous sweaters with Rudolph on the front.

Although tonight her little black dress doesn't look wholesome at all. It looks like a little piece of cloth I'd like to remove with my teeth. And after hearing her conversation with her friend, that possibility might just be the perfect way to top off what's already a good night.

Especially with my brother's marriage to Briar.

I gesture to the barman, who, of course, works for Moretti Global, since this nightclub is part of our real estate portfolio, among the many others we own in the city.

Not that this woman seems to know who I am, which is perfect for me. I don't like women chasing me because of what I can offer them—money, power—even if that power has a dirty little history we'd all like to forget.

The low amber lights above the bar cast a warm glow across the counter, catching the shine of bottles and glassware.

"Another beer?" the barman asks.

"Yeah, thanks." He slides my drink across the bar before going off to serve others. "So," I say, turning toward Pumpkin. "About this dilemma of yours. Who is the guy you think won't allow you to walk tomorrow? Consider me intrigued."

She goes bright red, her eyes wide and clear as they look up at me. Green— the greenest eyes—reminding me of Ireland, a place close to my heart, simply because it isn't the craziness and busyness of this city. Which I also love, but my cottage in County Cork does keep me sane whenever I need to get away.

She bites her lip, and I can see she's hesitating. The weight behind that trepidation makes me even more curious. Maybe it's me she's been ogling and hoping to be the one to fuck her. I'd be more than willing to make her walk tomorrow a little less comfortable.

"Actually, it's you."

I raise my brows, surprised she would out herself right away. I thought she would play it a little less forward and tell me it's someone else. The idea of her fucking any other rando in the club makes my lip curl, and I take a sip of beer to remind myself this woman is a stranger. Not someone I know or care for. I sure as fuck shouldn't give two shits whom she fucks.

"You want me to fuck you until you can't walk? Are we clear on the rules?"

It's her turn to choke on her drink, which looks like pop. "Is that vodka and orange? I think your drink stepped out of the nineties."

A smile breaks over her plump lips, and I grind my teeth, unable now to not think about what they would look like wrapped around my cock. After all, she's brought up the conversation regarding sex. It's no wonder my mind has well and truly landed in the gutter.

"I like vodka and orange. I'm not a big drinker."

I nod and wait for her to answer my first question. When she doesn't, I ask again. "So, about us fucking. You in?"

Her attention dips to my chest, and like a physical caress, moves up my body. I see her eyes narrow on my tats, on my shoulders, before she raises her pretty face to mine. She's interested and eager—I can see it in her features—but will she act on those emotions?

I lean down, clasp her about her nape, and wrench her against me. She slams into me, her breasts pressing hard against my chest, making my cock hard. I dip my head, give her a chance to pull away, to protest, before I kiss the fuck out of those sweet lips that I've been wanting against mine for the past ten minutes.

She doesn't push me away.

Perfect. My cue.

She tastes like vodka and morning juice—sour, and yet I know she'll be sweet. Our tongues tangle, and I hear her moan, her body molding to my every muscle. I reach down and clasp her ass, lift her against my cock, and kiss her deep while I grind her against me. She relents, goes limp, her fingers tangling into my hair, fisting my locks and pinning me against her.

I'm not going anywhere—unless it's in a car where I can get her alone and fuck the shit out of this Pumpkin.

I pull back and move away, picking up my beer—anything but to reach for her again and lift her onto the bar and eat her sweet pussy in front of everyone. I know she's wet for me; I can almost smell her desire, and it's a fragrance close to my heart.

Somewhere behind us, the DJ shifts tracks, the

beat dropping heavier and making the crowd erupt in cheers.

She stares at me, a little confused, and I grin, taking a deep swig of my drink. "You okay, Pumpkin? You seem a little dazed, but since you were hesitating, I thought a kiss might help you make up your mind a little quicker. I'm eager to start if you are."

"I'm Dallen."

I chuckle, having not asked her name, and yet I can't help it. In her confusion, she thinks I may want to know. Of course I do, but it isn't essential information. I hold out my hand. "Nice to meet you, Dallen. I'm Stephen."

"Okay, great." She reaches for her drink and downs it with one swallow. "Now that we're introduced, let's fuck."

THREE

DALLEN

WHAT AM I DOING? I WAVE GOODBYE TO AMY, WHO salutes me with her glass of wine, before I take Stephen's hand and start toward where I think the exit is to this nightclub. I haven't been here much in the past, not being much of a party girl.

Case in point, why I'm still carrying around my V-card. Even so, I think I'm going in the right direction and hope the little gumption the alcohol has given me lasts until I fuck the man who's holding my hand and making me feel all kinds of tingly.

I don't know how I managed to score a guy who looks devastatingly fucking hot and built who seems more than willing to do what I want for my first, but I have, and now I have to go through with it.

No, you don't, Dallen. You can leave whenever you want.

I know that's true, but I so want to experience what I feel like I've been missing out on. A connection with another person that I've not been able to take part in, mostly due to my parents—my father in particular—and his possessiveness over everything in my life. Understandable after the death of my brother Daniel due to getting caught in the crossfire of a gang killing he'd been assigned to that went wrong.

I push the thought of my brother away. I can't be sad tonight. Tonight I'm a little tipsy, and I'm going to use that bolster to my confidence to fuck the shit out of this hot dude who seems willing to scratch the itch I have.

A cool draft from the hallway brushes over my bare legs as we near the doors, the change in temperature snapping my senses awake. I debate my decision all the way to the nightclub doors. Fuck the shit out of him? Who am I kidding? This is probably going to hurt, and I'll end up regretting my life choices in the morning. But at least I won't die a virgin and will have ticked off another one of life's gifts that I promised myself I would do before turning twenty-nine.

Stephen steps out in front of me just as I'm about to hail a cab and gestures up the street. A car's lights turn on before the black vehicle pulls up to the nightclub. Stephen reaches for the door and opens it for me.

"You have a car?" I ask.

"I have lots of things." He grins and gestures for me to get in.

I look into the vehicle. It seems clean enough, and the driver is an elderly man who looks over his shoulder and gives me a friendly smile. I smile back, wondering how many other women Stephen has brought into this very vehicle over the years.

Probably more than he could count on his hands.

"Are you going to get in, or are we not going to fuck as you asked me?"

I feel the heat kiss my cheeks, and I gape at Stephen. Did he truly just say that out loud? Loud enough for the driver to hear and anyone standing close enough to us on the street? I hear someone behind us clear his throat, and I turn to see the bouncer trying to hide a grin.

I purse my lips. So he heard. I lift my chin, not willing to let him know I'm hoping the earth will open up and swallow me whole right about now. "Of course. I was just ensuring the car was clean, which it is, so that's fine." I inwardly groan at my absurd excuse for hesitating and climb into the back of the car, shuffling to the other side before the creak of leather tells me that Stephen has followed. "64th St, Lenox Hill, please," I advise the driver.

The door shuts, and the interior light turns off. I swallow as the sound of the city is muted, and all I'm left with is the sound of my heart beating in my ears. I can feel Stephen's heat beside me, his strength, and his scent, *Oud of Gods* if I'm not incorrect, smells delicious.

Outside the window, neon signs streak into colored blurs, giving the whole moment a dreamlike edge. The car pulls easily out into traffic, and for several heart-beats, I think he won't say anything. Shouldn't we talk some more? Get to know each other?

The feel of his hand slipping onto my leg startles me at first, but in for a penny, in for a pound—I don't remove his hand. Instead, I pretend to be someone I'm not. I turn to look at him and fight not to sigh in plea-sure when I find him watching me with an intensity that leaves the hairs on the back of my neck prickling.

He's so intense, so goddamn good-looking I ache at the very sight of him. His hand squeezes my thigh and slips closer toward where my panties are. Boldly, I open my legs. How I have the ovaries to do such a thing, I have no idea. This isn't me. I don't do these kinds of things. I'm a good girl. I do as I'm told and what I'm asked, and that's the end of my life.

But here and now, tonight, I don't want to be a good girl. I want this man to make me a woman. I want to feel what it's like to be taken, to be owned by a man.

I want to feel everything.

"Naughty girl... You surprise me, Pumpkin."

I surprise myself. "Do I?" I say instead, wanting to sound as confident as my body is portraying me to be. "What else can I do for you other than surprise?"

Stephen reaches for the door and presses a button, and a screen that shields us from the driver goes up, leaving us cocooned in the backseat. He raises his brows and moves to face me. His hand slips up the last of my thigh, tickling my skin before his fingers skim ever so lightly over my mons. I suck in a startled breath. I've touched myself, of course. I've orgasmed from my own fingers, but this... This is far more intense and intimate.

I'm allowing a stranger access to my most private of places and spreading my legs to let him know he can have me.

"So wet already." He wrenches my panties aside and slips his fingers into me.

I reach for him, needing to ground myself in some way lest I lose control of where and who I am. "Stephen." His name is a moan on my lips, but I can't hold it back. His fingers stretch me, tease me as he works them in and out.

"That feels so good." I spread my legs wider just as his thumb circles my clit while he fucks me with his fingers. I groan and throw my head back. I stare at the car's roof, the city lights from the skyscrapers illuminate the vehicle.

His mouth nuzzles my throat, and I clasp the nape of his neck, holding him against me. I'm lost in a sea of lights and enlightenment, and I couldn't want him more than I do right at this moment.

Sex has always scared me. The thought of it is probably one of the reasons why I've waited so long, but with Stephen, the way my body reacts to the very sight of him tells me that it's time.

Stephen slips onto his knees. He throws me a wicked smirk that leaves me achingly wet before he spreads my legs and reaches up my short dress to rip off my panties. He lifts them to his face, takes a deep breath, and groans.

"You smell as sweet as you'll taste." He slips his fingers into his mouth, sucking the digits that just a moment before were inside me. I know I'm gaping. I probably look like some stunned deer in headlights at everything he's doing, but I can't help myself.

This is all new to me.

"Put your legs on my shoulders, Pumpkin."

I take a deep breath, having read of the position but never having imagined I would get my turn to try it.

I lift my legs and slip them over his shoulders. He clasps my ass and wrenches me down farther on the seat. My dress falls to my waist, and I can see that from the waist down, I'm open and exposed to him. My legs spread, my pussy his to observe in all its glory.

Well, I hope he's thinking of it in such a way...

"Beautiful." He dips his head, and the feel of his tongue as it slides up between my wet folds makes me buck. The sensation is like nothing I've ever experienced before. It's everything and more, all rolled into one.

His tongue teases me, flicks my clit before sucking hard.

"Stephen." I gasp his name, press myself against him like some wanton hussy. But oh, this is the sweetest torture that I never want to end.

"Fuck you taste good. I'm going to eat your fucking cunt before I fuck the shit out of you."

"Yes." I want him so much. I feel a rush of liquid, and he groans, pressing two of his fingers into me again before adding a third.

The pressure is a little uncomfortable, but nice—nothing I can't handle—and the more he stretches me, the better it feels. He twists his hand to a different angle and rolls his finger somewhere deep inside that sends a profound, throbbing pressure building within me.

"Oh fuck yeah," I moan, rolling my hips, wanting him deeper, harder.

"I need to fuck you. I want to wait, but I need to have you here. Now."

"Yes." I want nothing more. I forget my fear of

what is to come and instead revel in the sight of him as he straightens and rips open his jeans, unzipping his pants. His cock catapults into his hand, and he watches me watch him stroke his cock.

He's hugeeeee.

I meet his eyes, and I know he knows what I'm thinking.

"It'll fit. I promise."

I nod and bite my lip, waiting for him. He wrenches me to the edge of the seat and presses his cock against the entrance of my cunt. The feel of him there is nice, like my body knows what it wants and craves without ever knowing why.

"I'm going to watch myself stretch your beautiful pussy."

I wrap my legs about his waist, feeling warmth yet again gush between my legs. Just him talking to me makes me horny, makes me eager for whatever else he has in store for me.

He clasps the tops of my thighs and presses into me. He's huge, and I fear he's not going to fit.

"Breathe, Dallen. I'll fit. I promise."

I nod and try not to freeze up. He stops pressing into me and rolls his thumb over my clit. I'm transported immediately to pleasure, to forgetting the uncomfortable pressure between my thighs, and instead, the feel of him inside me and him teasing me with his fingers is too much and yet not enough.

"I feel so full, so achingly full."

"You'll feel better soon—I promise you that. I'm going to make you come on my cock." He leans down and kisses me for the second time. I need this to want him so much. He kisses me deep and long, his tongue teasing mine as slowly I feel him press all the way into me.

"That's it, beautiful. I'm in... Now for the fun part."

FOUR

STEPHEN

She's so tight, a perfect fit. My balls ache, and I want to come, but I won't. Not yet, but soon. Very soon.

Never have I seen such a beautiful sight as the one that lies before me. Dallen is stunning, hot as fuck, and so goddamn responsive that just the thought of having her makes me take things in the car a little further than I should. I could at least make it back to my apartment.

I'll owe my driver an apology and a beer after this.

But no. Here I am, fucking a woman I met at the bar half an hour ago and with no damn regrets about it. I thrust into her and she moans, her fingers digging into my hair. I like the pain. I want to feel more of it, if it means I'm bringing her pleasure.

"That's it, Pumpkin. Take all of me."

She makes a sweet mewling sound, and damn it all

to hell, I struggle not to spend early. My balls ache, and never has my cock been so hard, so ready to explode. I lean back and watch her take my meat. She stretches with each thrust, her cunt writhing and pulling at my dick until I think I can't stand it a moment longer.

"Stephen..."

My name on her lips has me pull free. I'll come if I listen to her husky, whispered words a moment longer and stay deep at the same time. I slump onto the seat beside her, and she turns to look at me. I can see the need, the desperation in her eyes for us to continue. I will, of course, but I need a moment.

Jesus, I'm like a virgin all over again. Two pumps and I'll come.

"Come and sit on my lap," I order her. At least with that position, she can control the depth, the speed at which we fuck. I have less control, and sometimes that is hotter than me fucking a woman until I hear her scream.

"On your lap?" She moves, even though I hear the question in her words. She straddles my legs, and I clasp her ass, hoisting her up against my cock. She rubs against me, teases her wet cunt against my hard-as-fuck cock, and I close my eyes, grit my teeth, and pray not to spill all over her pretty black dress before I hear her sweet cry of release.

"Like this?"

"Yeah, just like that, baby. Lift yourself up on your knees, I'll help guide myself into you."

"So I get to be in control?" she says.

I grin—how could I not? She's so sweet and innocent and hot as fuck. "Yes, you get to control the game now."

She makes a humming sound of delight and lifts her pert ass up high enough for me to set my cock at her entrance. With a slowness that almost deprives me of sense, she lowers herself onto my dick.

Inch by inch, I impale her. Her tight cunt wraps around my cock, and I take a deep breath, fighting for my life and sanity. She lowers herself on me before rising again. Over and over, she does that same wicked flex of her hips that makes me want to flip her onto her back again and take her hard and long.

Damn, where has this woman come from? Tonight won't be enough. I want more of her.

"That's it, beautiful. Fuck the shit out of me."

She nods but doesn't say a word, merely speeding up her movements and taking me deeper. I can feel myself stretching her. Hell, she's tight—perfect.

I can't get enough of her.

I want to eat her up.

Again.

The desire teases my mind, but before I can act on it, I feel the tightening of her sweet cunt.

"Stephen!" she screams, her fingers diving through my hair, pulling me close. I kiss her deep and long and relish the feel of her orgasm as it convulses around my cock. I somehow manage to hold off joining her before she slumps against my chest, pliant and panting heavily.

I move her hair off her shoulder and kiss her neck. She smells just as good as I think—like vanilla and sex.

Outside the windows, the glow of passing street-lights streaks softly across her skin, turning every movement into something molten and slow.

The car pulls up to a tall building, and I glance out the window. Her stop. I make a note of the building, slipping it into my memory as I wait for her to realize the car has stopped.

"You're home," I announce, unable to stop the grin twisting my lips as she stills in my arms and looks around.

"Oh gosh, I didn't know." She slips off me, and I suck in a breath, my cock still hard, my balls aching to join her in her pleasure. "Thank you for giving me a lift back to my place."

"Which ride are you thanking me for?" I want to tease her, to see her pretty cheeks blossom in pink. But there is nothing dirty or wrong with a quick fuck in the back of a car by two consenting adults.

Tonight will not be the last for us.

She wiggles her panties back on to her sweet ass and settles her dress about her knees. "Both, I suppose." She leans forward and kisses me.

I take the opportunity to devour her mouth. I want her; my cock lies hard and ready in my lap. I know she can see it, and once more she surprises me. She reaches down and strokes her finger along my length. It jerks under her touch, and she throws me a mischievous grin.

"Goodnight, Stephen..." She pulls away, and I let her go. Just. I want to wrench her back into the car as she opens the door and climbs out as if nothing has happened within the confined space. I'm legless and hard as hell, aching for more. But I can wait. I'm a patient man—for some things—and something tells me that I'll wait as long as I need to have sweet little Dallen in my arms again.

In my bed.

Where she belongs.

FIVE

STEPHEN

THE LOFT GREETS ME THE WAY IT ALWAYS DOES—
quiet, grounded, familiar.

Warm walnut floors stretch beneath my feet. Their
grain catches the low amber light from recessed fixtures
tucked into the beams overhead. Exposed brick lines one
wall. Floating shelves are stacked with books I've actually read, and a few I pretend I have. Old ledgers, framed
black-and-white photographs of the city before it was
polished and sold to the highest bidder. Steel and glass
make appearances where needed. But they don't domi-
nate. Nothing here feels cold. Nothing screams excess.

People don't expect that from a Moretti.

They expect black marble, chrome, and sharp
angles. Something that looks like it could cut you if you
leaned too close. Instead, my place looks lived in.

Intentional. A bachelor's home that doesn't feel like a showroom or a threat.

I know the moment I step out of the elevator, I'm not alone. I reach over to my hallstand, open the drawer, and pull out my pistol. The caution is unwarranted when I spy Lucien, my brother, seated on the leather sectional, one ankle crossed over his knee, jacket off, sleeves rolled. A glass of whiskey sits in his hand as if it's an extra appendage to his body.

He smirks. "You're late. More wrinkled than at the club."

I tug at the knot of my tie, loosening it, then peel off my jacket and drape it over the back of a chair. "I had a good night."

"So I can see."

I roll my shoulders, tension still humming through me. It's not from the club's crowded energy, but from the quiet, lingering adrenaline of the car ride after. Thoughts of Dallen's mouth, her hands, return. The memory feels different—warmer, more personal. The fear that letting anyone close could threaten the careful life I've built, or theirs, sharpens it. Her gaze—the way she looked at me like I wasn't just a name whispered in rooms after I'd walked out—sticks with me. It presses at something vulnerable I keep hidden, reminding me what I have to lose.

I pour myself a drink. "You been waiting long? Shouldn't you be home with Briar?"

"She's out with Stacy for a little while longer. I thought I'd come here and see what you're up to since I lost track of you." He pauses. "But I've been here long enough to finish one glass and convince myself you weren't dead, merely having fun." Lucien lifts his whiskey in a mock toast. "Congratulations, brother. Now... Who was the lay?"

I snort and pour myself a drink before joining him on the couch, sinking into the leather. It creaks softly beneath my weight, worn in all the right places. Comfortable, old, and well used.

A faint hum from the HVAC kicks on above us, the cool air drifting down and stirring the edge of a paper on the coffee table.

Lucien's eyes flick to my glass, then back to my face. He's smiling. Not the calculated, terrifying smile people fear. The real one. The one Briar put back on to his lips.

I change the subject. "Letting Briar out of your sight? You must be getting soft."

His face softens. "Not soft. She's safe and having fun. I'll see her in a couple of hours. There's nothing soft about me."

I scoff and sip my whiskey. "You're insufferable."

He shrugs. "Yup. She was worth it."

We both know what that means. Matteo Romero doesn't breathe anymore. Lucien's choice—love over restraint—echoes through us. He chooses Briar over law and order, over the right way to do things. The consequences reverberate, not just in the city, but in me. In that moment, anger, fear, and longing all collide. Our father never taught us to handle that. The decision shows me what's really at stake: losing yourself for someone, or losing them by playing it safe.

And something tells me I would do the same if I were in love as much as my brother seems to be—a flicker of realization passing through me at the thought.

"The charity auction at the Met is coming up again. Committee wants confirmations this week."

Lucien nods. "We'll have them. The foundation already secured five major donors from last year alone."

"Six. Dutch family confirmed. Same table, same donation."

Lucien hums in approval. "Good. I want to break last year's total."

"That was seven figures."

"I know."

"That's ambitious." But not impossible. When it came to my brother and the connections our family had built up over the past ten years, he was capable of anything.

"So was surviving our childhood," he says mildly. "And yet, here we are."

I sip, steadying. "Security's tighter, fewer unknowns. Should be a good night."

"Briar wants to be more visible this year."

My sister-in-law spent the past year working to distance herself from her murdered ex-husband. Now, she's becoming the face of Moretti Global's charity side. If the public ever learns Lucien Moretti rid the world of Matteo Romero, none of us would recover. We'd lose everything. "As she should be," I say. "People trust her."

"They adore her," Lucien corrects. "And they should."

I glance at his hand—a custom wedding ring. Understated. Lethal in value, if you knew what to look for. "I never thought I'd see you like this," I admit. A small part of me wants what my brother has. The way he looks at Briar immortalizes her with every glance. I can't help but be jealous of such love. A bond of unbreakable trust. "Happy?"

He smirks. "Yeah, I am."

I'm happy for him, and can only hope that one day I'll have that same fortune in love. "You're almost human now," I tease. "Who would have thought?"

He laughs. "Careful. That talk gets you killed."

"In our old circles, perhaps. We're making new ones now."

We sit in companionable silence for a moment, the city humming beyond the tall windows. Taxis. Sirens. Life. A distant horn echoes up from the street, bouncing between the buildings before fading into the night.

Then Lucien shifts, turning slightly toward me. "So," he says casually. "The redhead at the bar. Was that the enjoyable night? Is she someone I need to know more about?"

I freeze for exactly half a second.

He grins, not missing a beat. "You know, the one you left with. Tall, Siren's hair, didn't care about your name."

I exhale and sink deeper into the couch. "You always watching?"

"Always," he says. "And judging by the state of your shirt..." His gaze flicks to the faint crease across my chest. "The ride home was...productive."

I scoff. "I don't divulge details."

"I didn't ask for them." He grins. "But I approve."

I hide a smile. "It ended pleasantly."

"Mm."

"And I hope to see her again," I admit, not really knowing why I want my brother to know that fact.

Lucien stands, setting down his glass. "It's about

time." He claps my shoulder. "Good to see a spark again, Stephen."

I swallow, nodding once.

He pauses at the door, one hand on the elevator button. "Try not to scare her off."

The elevator opens and closes before him, leaving the loft silent again. I sit there for a long moment, staring at the space he occupied, a heaviness settling in my chest. His words echo—a spark. With a jolt, I realize how dim everything had become until tonight. Until Dallen.

I pull my phone from my pocket, thumb hovering before I type her first name into the search bar along with her address.

Nothing.

No surname hint. No socials. No tagged photos. No digital trail.

That's...unusual. I lean back and exhale slowly, confusion mixing with relief. It's a reminder of the risks. People disappear when they learn who I am, who our father was, and the chaos he inflicted on the city in the eighties. What hell our name carries. Every connection feels dangerous, as though honesty would ruin any hope of happiness.

Dallen doesn't know anything about me. I should feel relieved that I may not see her again, but uncertainty twists in me. A part of me wants to keep what we've started uncomplicated for just a little longer, because the truth tends to scare people away. I can't decide which frightens me more—being rejected for what I am, or never being known at all.

And I don't think I'm ready to watch her walk. But as luck would have it, I know where she lives, so hope cuts through my uncertainty, settling a little anticipation in my chest.

I will see her again, and this time I'll find out her last name and number.

SIX

DALLEN

I walk into my parents' Tribeca apartment. It's opulent—old money meets working class, with my father as Chief of Police. I hear them in the upstairs parlor, my mother's favorite room, the cook humming in the kitchen as she prepares our usual Sunday roast. My mother always wished she'd been born into British aristocracy—apparently, that would've made her nearly perfect life even better.

"Mom, Dad, I'm home." I climb the stairs and enter the parlor to find them fussing over a painting that's leaning up against the wall, their debate clearly on where to place yet another masterpiece in the room.

"Darling, you're home. You're a little late. I wasn't sure if you remembered."

I roll my eyes, kiss my mother's cheeks, and hug my

father. "Mom, as if I'd forget roast night! We've done this every week since I was born."

"Yes, a bit traditional," she says, turning back to her painting. Dad settles on the settee, patting the seat. "Sit with me."

"What's new, buttercup? Did you actually go out last night?"

"I did." I swallow, hoping my father doesn't notice the warmth in my cheeks. I did more than just go out— I lost my virginity in the back of a car, and I can't regret it. A shiver runs through me. I enjoyed every second, and already I want more.

Why didn't I get his number or give him mine? In my rush to appear worldly, I left without sharing my details. I hope he wants to see me again. I'd only told him my first name—he'd never find me online.

That was probably a good thing. If he knew my dad was Chief of Police, he'd probably run. Most men were scared off when they found out, and when I brought anyone home, Dad made sure they knew who was boss. No wonder it took me so long to lose the big V.

But what a way to lose it. He was big, powerful, and made me come so hard I'm still dizzy twelve hours later. I shift, craving him, that sweet ache only he seems able to satisfy—or inflame.

From the hallway, footsteps tap the wooden floors

as one of the staff members moves briskly toward the kitchen.

"So, did you meet anyone?" Dad asks.

I meet my father's eyes. He's watching closely. I nod. "I did." I can't help the grin creeping in. "He's sinfully handsome. Drove me home—like a gentleman."

"As long as that's all he did, then I'm happy for you."

I frown. "Dad, don't be gross."

He lifts his hands in surrender. "You just met him, and he's already driving you home?"

"Well, actually, his driver drove me home."

"Oh? Someone we might know? What's his family name?" my mother asks, pausing her painting shuffle.

I hesitate, ignoring my father's narrowed eyes. "I can't remember. I had too much to drink, but I'm here, I'm safe, and he wasn't anyone important." *For you*, I didn't add. "Can we please change the subject?"

"Of course," my mother says with a warning look at Dad. "But if you see him again, invite him over. I'd like to meet anyone who catches your eye. For a moment, I worried you might be a lesbian."

I take a deep breath. "Enough, Mother. You can't say things like that. And if I loved someone of the same sex, you'd still love me, right?"

She arches a brow and calls for tea from the live-in staff.

The clink of china being arranged on a tray drifts up from the kitchen. I count the minutes until I can leave. My mother irritates me, and my father still treats me like a child who can't date—ridiculous, given I'm twenty-eight. I'm old enough to make my own choices, good or bad.

Mother pours tea into fine china cups. "Did you get that Dior gown I sent over this week? It'll be perfect for the Met Gala next week. Matches your eyes beautifully."

I nod, taking a sip of tea. "It's beautiful, Mother, and I'll wear it. But please, don't try to matchmake me with anyone at the event. If you do, I won't go. I can handle my own dates and decide whom I like."

"So you have a date lined up?" she asks sweetly— too sweetly.

"I'm going alone, which is perfectly fine." I hold her gaze until she offers me a thin smile.

"Very good. We'll make it a family night. It'll be nice to be together again now that you're based full-time in New York. We missed you when you were living in Los Angeles. Dreadful, hot place."

Oh, to be back in the City of Angels again. "Yes, we'll have a splendid time," I say, sarcasm lacing my words. My father glares at me, and I smile back.

Maybe I could ask my law firm to send me back to LA. Wishful thinking. They needed me in New York, and I knew I wouldn't be going anywhere for some time. More's the pity.

The savory scent of roasted garlic drifts in from the kitchen. We move to the dining room. My mother launches into gossip—who wore what at her weekly friends' lunch, who embarrassed themselves, and which family might be having financial trouble. I nod, my mind drifting as I eat a potato, and her voice fades into background noise.

All I can think about is Stephen.

The way he'd kissed me like he meant it.

The way he touched me like he'd known my body for years.

The way I still feel tender and trembling in the best possible way.

My mother is midway through a story when I realize I'm smiling at my plate. I clear my throat and sip my glass of wine, hoping no one notices my blush.

My father occasionally glances at me, curious, maybe suspicious, but he says nothing. Their chatter blurs—names, rumors, trivialities. My thoughts drift back to last night. To Stephen. To how alive I feel.

I take another sip of wine and set down my glass, my heart beating just a fraction faster.

Because whatever last night was...

I want more.

SEVEN

STEPHEN

I sit in my car and wait. I have no driver today, having been down in this part of New York for a real estate business meeting, and I thought I'd look in and see if Dallen happened to come and go from her building. I've been here for an hour already. Not that I'll tell her that—I'm not a stalker...yet—but I want to see her again. Already, the blood in my veins pumps fast at the thought of having her sweetness in my arms again.

These thoughts went against everything I am, what I was raised to be. Lucien fought hard to keep us younger siblings out of the life our father lived, but the old man always found a way. I'd seen things that Lucien didn't even know of, and I hope never learned about. I had been my father's right-hand kid, not man, kid far too often to count. I frown, hating the memory of what I did. Of what I'm capable of. When Lucien had killed Matteo Romero, that old surge of hate, of fury had risen within me, and had he asked—had he not been able to rid the world of that disease—I certainly would have. No questions asked. No hesitation.

I hoped that now my father's ruthlessness only came out in me through business deals. I rarely relented if I wanted something and always got what I wanted in the end. That aggression was the same when it came to women. I always got what I wanted.

Dallen would be no different. I convince myself I want her because I always get what I want, but with her there's a nagging worry—maybe it's more than just wanting. Maybe it's about needing someone to see past what I am.

I see her. Finally. She's wearing black trousers and a white silk shirt. She has a bouquet of flowers in her arms. What ass bought her those? I look around, knowing I didn't bring anything for her. I should have. Rookie mistake. She stops walking and looks down at her phone, and smiles at whatever notification she received. Maybe she was seeing someone? She didn't mention anyone when I was fucking her in my car. When she was coming down hard on my cock and driving me insane.

I check my mirrors, step out, and block her path.

She doesn't see me—walks straight into me. A soft "oomph" escapes her lips. She looks up, recognizes me, and the pleasure on her face gives me hope. I glance at the flowers before meeting her eyes.

"Hello, Dallen." I soak in her presence. She's even prettier up close in daylight. I want to pull her to me, breathe her in—fruit and summer, tropical. I don't know why I crave her, it's not normal for me.

"Stephen." Her words are breathless, as if the sight of me leaves her stunned, excited. I hope it does.

"I didn't think to see you again." A blush steals over her cheeks, and I know she's remembering our time in the car and what we did. What I want to do to her again.

"Are you free? I want to take you out for dinner if you're available?"

She looks around, hesitating. Maybe she doesn't want to go out. I could eat her instead if she prefers. "Only if you want to. No pressure. We did meet—and get to know each other—fast, but it was...satisfying and strange."

Her laugh and genuine smile give me hope. "I don't have any plans tonight, so of course I'd love to. But I have to go upstairs first and drop off my flowers." She hesitates. "Would you like to come up?"

"Sure." I look up at the building, one of the oldest in New York, renovated into apartments and sold off to individuals. Only those with money lived in them, and although it was several stories high, it was one of the most- sought-after apartment blocks in NY since it allowed each apartment holder private access to the park across the road. I'd been trying to purchase into the building for years without success. "Have you lived here long? This building is one I've often admired."

The building rises from the street like a relic, carved stone and quiet grandeur, as if Manhattan grew up around it. Its façade shows old money—arched sandstone-framed windows, aged wrought-iron balconies, and a broad entrance crowned by an elegant portico. Time has refined it, not diminished it.

She enters her pin and the door unlocks before we enter the foyer, and she presses the elevator button. "A while. This was my mother's flat before she married my father, but it's mine now." She shrugs. "Lucky, I guess."

I follow Dallen into the elevators, surprised to find the doors open into a private foyer when we reach her floor. Heavy doors greet us that look like they've been opened and closed a thousand times before. The building has the same bones as mine—solid, old, unapologetic. None of that glass-and-steel nonsense that makes every apartment feel like a hotel suite you're only meant to stay in temporarily.

Her place opens into a feeling of warmth. Dark wood floors stretch out beneath my feet, worn just enough to tell a story. A plush lounge sits opposite a low table layered with books and throw rugs in muted colors, the kind that invite you to sit, sink, stay awhile. Framed paintings line the walls—landscapes, abstracts, something that looks like it might've been done by a family member rather than a gallery. It feels lived in. Loved.

"This is me," Dallen says, slipping off her shoes.

Before I can respond, a blur of fur launches itself from the back of the sofa.

"Well, hello," I mutter as a black cat trots over like it owns the place.

"This is Puss Puss," Dallen says fondly. She drops to her knees without hesitation, kisses the top of her cat's head, and scratches behind her ears. "She thinks she's in charge."

Puss Puss blinks at me, unimpressed.

"Fair," I say.

Dallen laughs, rising. "I'm just going to change. Make yourself comfortable."

She disappears down the hall, leaving behind the faint scent of her perfume and something else—home. I watch her walk away, wanting her more with every second I'm in her presence. I shouldn't want her as much as I do. She's sweet and seems far too intelligent to date a Moretti, but still, I can't shift my feet to leave. To let her go and not take a chance on a man who could possibly never give her the safety she deserves. Not with our history and enemies. There was always a risk.

I wander into the lounge, hands in my pockets, taking in the space slowly. A bookshelf filled with dog-eared novels and framed photos catches my attention. Her family. Smiling faces. Holiday snapshots. A younger Dallen and an older boy between two people I assume are her parents, her grin wide and unguarded. There's love there. Stability. The kind of roots I've never had.

I'm studying a beach photo of her when footsteps sound. I turn, taking a steadying breath.

Dallen stands, transformed yet still herself. A soft floral dress flatters her; a light jacket over her shoulders adds elegance. Hair, loose and framing her face, makes my chest tighten. Flat shoes—sensible. Perfect.

She shifts, suddenly shy under my stare. "Too much or not enough?"

I cross the distance between us in two strides, stopping just short of touching her. "No," I say quietly. "You look...beautiful."

Color blooms in her cheeks, her smile slow and genuine. "Ready for dinner?" she asks.

I nod, offering my arm. "Very."

We head back out together, the door closing softly behind us, and for the first time in a long while, I find myself looking forward to what comes next.

The restaurant Delizioso is the kind of place that makes you feel like you should lower your voice the second you step inside—but as the owner, I know it's the perfect location for a first date. I have my own table, always available, no matter when I turn up. Dark wood. White tablecloths. Low, golden light that catches on the rim of wine glasses and turns everything a little softer. The host greets me by name, which is always a convenient perk of being one of the bosses.

The soft clatter of cutlery blends with low conversation. Dallen walks in beside me, and I keep my hand at the small of her back as we're led through the dining room. I take in who's dining already, not seeing anyone of interest or anyone who shouldn't be here.

"Is it terrible that I'm impressed?" she murmurs, looking about, pleasure on her features as she takes in the restaurant. "I've wanted to eat here for some time, but the place is booked out like a year in advance."

I glance at her, amused. "I aim to please."

"Clearly," she says, like it's the most obvious statement in the world.

A smile tugs at my mouth. "You don't know me well enough to be impressed yet."

Her eyes flick up at me, daring. "I know enough."

That hits lower than it should. Does she mean from

our one-night stand, or has she tried to find more about me? I didn't give her my surname. A Google search for the Moretti name yields far too much information for any potential partner to absorb after a first meeting. My family needed to be introduced gradually, over time...not right away.

We sit. A waiter glides over like he's got a stick along his spine and sets water down, offers the menu, and goes through the suggestions for this evening's meals before giving us some privacy to decide.

Dallen opens her menu, brows lifting as she reads what's available. "Okay, I officially feel like I should've worn something fancier."

"You look perfect," I say without thinking. And she does—good enough for this restaurant or any other. I drink in the sight of her, wanting her with a need that's foreign to me. I ache to kiss her, to lean across the small distance that separates us and merely kiss her sweet lips. The thought sweeps through me, and I don't know who the fuck I am when I'm around her.

She pauses. Looks up. Something soft flickers across her face, like she's deciding whether to accept the compliment or tease me for it.

"Careful," she says. "If you keep talking like that, I'm going to start thinking you're a nice guy."

I lean back in my chair, letting my gaze linger. "And if I am?" Which, of course, is true to a point. I am a nice guy. I work hard, I play by the rules most of the time at work and in my family, but there is a line. Like all my brothers, we are perfectly content until someone crosses that line, and then all bets are off. I know I have it in me—the revenge, the fury that comes forth if something I care about is threatened.

"Then I'll have to reevaluate my whole opinion of men who do one-night stands. Perhaps there's absolution for them after all. So far, you're giving those guys a good name."

I laugh under my breath. "If I recall, I don't believe I forced you into my car."

"No, you didn't," she says immediately. "But you did use your sexy-as-hell face to tempt me to misbehave in a way that I wouldn't normally. In a way that I never have before."

I freeze at her words, remembering back to that night, of showering when I returned home, and the blood on my cock. I should have worn a condom, but in the heat of the moment, shit happens. But the blood? I'd thought the force with which I'd taken her had caused a little too much friction, but was I wrong?

"Hang on." The blood pumps loudly in my ears at the realization that I'd possibly been her first. That she'd trusted me enough to give me the honor. I shouldn't be trusted with something so precious. I could turn on a dime—I knew it down in my bones. I was as ruthless as my father and my siblings when the need arose. But this... "You were a virgin?" I pause, can feel the frown between my brows. "Was I your first?"

She shrugs and bites into a buttered piece of bread the waiter brought over to the table. "That's unimportant semantics." Her lips twitch as if she knows that's not true at all. "Also, I'm pretty sure you didn't even know I was, so what does it matter?"

Oh, it matters. It means I was her first, and knowing that makes me want to be her last.

The waiter returns, pausing our conversation, and asks if we want wine. Dallen's gaze darts to me, questioning.

"Give us a bottle of your best white," I suggest to the waiter, watching her, and no one else.

"Of course, sir. I'll source that now."

I meet the waiter's gaze. "Excellent."

"And have you decided on your meals this evening?"

We order. Decide on a shared appetizer because Dallen suggests it, and I want to please her. I like that she's comfortable around me. I may dress nicer than most, have money to burn, and a good job, but my appearance can sometimes be a little intimidating. My height, the tatts, the sharp jaw, and cold gaze. These features, however, don't seem to bother her. She doesn't seem to notice them at all. I like that. I like it more than I thought I would.

She rests her forearms on the table and watches me for a moment. "So, tell me about you."

The question is casual, like she's asking about the weather. But it isn't off-the-cuff. Not for me. I'm used to conversations where I know the rules. Where everyone is either trying to impress me, use me, or avoid offending me. Dallen doesn't do any of that. She's just curious. Like she assumes the truth is an option.

"I work," I say, intentionally vague.

She snorts. "Wow. Riveting."

I give her a look. "I'm captivating, I know."

Dallen's smile widens, and her eyes dip—quick and instinctive—to my mouth. The memory of her lips on mine flashes hot and immediate, like my body never got the memo that we're in public now.

She clears her throat, then tries again. "Okay, fine. What do you do for work?"

I'm about to answer—my job isn't a secret, but I also don't want her knowing my surname, something she'll surely learn if she knows my employment. I don't want to be vague, but I also need more time before she forms her opinion of me. I need her to get to know me first, before I'm tainted by my own family's history.

But just as I'm about to disclose my occupation,

movement near the restaurant door catches my attention.

It's subtle at first. Just a shift in the atmosphere, like the air in the room dims.

A man walks in with a purposeful stride, dressed in something that looks expensive but not in a showy way. Dark hair. Clean shave. A watch that costs more than most people's monthly rent. He doesn't scan the room like a tourist. He scans it like a predator.

My gaze locks on to him before I can stop myself.

A Romero.

Not Matteo—Matteo is gone. But the eyes are the same. The bone structure. The way the shoulders sit back like the world is supposed to move around him.

My jaw tightens.

The guy looks away, no emotion on his face, nothing to give away that he knows, in turn, who I am. But that doesn't mean anything. He could've already clocked me from the door. He could've picked this place because he knew I'd be here. That a Moretti is one of the owners. Or he could be here for someone else, and I'm just overly paranoid after Lucien offed Matteo.

He slides onto a stool at the bar, leans in toward the bartender, and says something with a smile. Normal. Casual. Like he's just another guy getting a drink before dinner.

I don't buy it.

"Stephen?" Dallen says, and I realize I've gone still and silent. "Hey. Are you okay?"

I blink, dragging my attention back to her. Her brows are pinched together, concern mixing with curiosity.

"Yeah," I lie. "Just...thinking."

"About what?"

I want to tell her the truth. That there's a Romero in the room and my brother's name lives like a ghost in their family tree now that he's married to Briar. That this could be nothing, or it could be the start of something ugly. That I'm doing math in my head. Exits, angles, who could be with him, who might be outside.

But the truth is a trap. Once you say it, you can't unsay it. And I don't know what Dallen would do with it.

She studies me, unimpressed by my vague answer. "Thinking about me?"

I almost smile at the out she offers me. "Always."

Her eyes narrow like she doesn't believe me, but her mouth betrays her—softening, pleased. "Okay," she says slowly. "Then let's talk about something less... mysterious. I'll go first and talk about my career. Since you dodged it."

"Go ahead," I say, even as my attention keeps snagging toward the bar. The Romero lifts his glass. Takes a sip. Laughs at something the bartender says.

Dallen tucks a strand of hair behind her ear. "I'm a lawyer."

The words hit like a glass dropped on marble. I keep my face neutral, but inside, everything shifts.

"A lawyer," I repeat carefully.

"Mm-hmm," she says. "Corporate litigation. Mostly. Sometimes personal cases, if they're the right fit. But I'm usually buried in contracts and disputes."

I nod. My throat feels tight. Not because she's a lawyer. Because of what that means if this—whatever this is—becomes real. The Moretti name doesn't come with clean edges. Not fully. Not even now, when we're "legitimate." There are always shadows. Always something that doesn't fit neatly into board meetings and charity galas.

And if something happens—if someone comes for us, if a deal goes bad, if there's retaliation or an accident or a body we never bet on—what would Dallen do with her conscience and her law degree and her belief in justice? What would she do if she found out I'm not just a guy who took her to dinner?

Her gaze flicks over my face, reading me too well. "Is that...a problem?"

"No," I say immediately, too fast.

Shit.

Dallen leans back slightly, like she's giving me space to either be honest or keep lying. "Stephen."

I glance at the bar again without meaning to. The Romero has turned a fraction, his profile visible. He's listening to something on his phone now, head tilted, smile fading.

I force myself to look at Dallen. "It's not a problem," I say again, slower. "It's just...unexpected."

"Why?"

Because lawyers come with questions. Because lawyers come with standards. Because lawyers come with a world I've never belonged to, even when I'm wearing a suit in a room full of people pretending we're all the same.

I lift my glass and take a sip of water I don't need. "What made you want to get into law?" I ask, buying time.

Dallen exhales, a little relieved that I'm engaging. "I like fixing things and arguing, so it's a good fit for my personality."

"You sound like you love it."

"It's everything to me," she counters. "Not everything can be fixed, but a lot can. And I'm good at my job and hope to make partner soon."

I nod, even as my mind runs through worst-case scenarios. If things go sideways, could she defend us?

Would she? Or would she look at me like I'm the kind of man she should've crossed the street to avoid?

Dallen's eyes soften. "What's going on in that head of yours right now?"

Too much. I let my gaze drop to her hands on the table. Clean nails. A simple ring. No flashy jewelry. Grounded. Real. I want to keep her in my life.

That's the problem.

I look up at her. "I'm trying to figure out if you're going to regret coming to dinner with me or if you'll give me a second chance."

Her lips part slightly. "That's what you're worried about? Another date after this one?"

I shrug, pretending it's casual. Pretending I'm not tracking the Romero like a loaded gun.

Dallen leans forward, voice lowering. "Stephen, I'm a grown woman. I don't do regrets because I had a good time with someone."

My chest tightens for a completely different reason. "And our time together?" I ask quietly. "Was it a good time?"

Her gaze drops to my mouth. "Our night was... more than a good time."

Heat curls low in my stomach, sharp and immediate.

Across the room, the Romero stands. My spine goes rigid.

He turns slightly, scanning the dining room now—slow, deliberate. His eyes pass over tables. Over faces. I keep my expression smooth, but inside, I'm already moving pieces on the board. Out of my peripheral vision, I see Dallen's gaze follow my line of sight, landing on the bar, then back to me.

"Is someone bothering you?" she asks, and there's steel in her voice now. Protective. Concern.

I swallow. If I tell her, I drag her into my world. If I don't tell her, I'm lying by omission—and I'm starting to realize she's the kind of woman who won't tolerate that for long. The Romero's gaze flicks in our direction for half a second and it's enough.

He knows I'm here.

I reach across the table, covering Dallen's hand with mine. "Finish what you were saying," I say softly, forcing a smile that I know doesn't reach my eyes. "Tell me how you got into law."

Dallen stares at me, unconvinced, but she doesn't pull away. "Stephen—"

"Please," I murmur, my thumb stroking the side of her hand like a promise and a warning all at once. "Just...tell me."

She watches me for another beat, then nods slowly, as if filing this moment away for later discussion. "Okay," she says, voice careful. "Well, it starts with my dad..."

And I listen. I really do. I listen to her words, the cadence of her voice, the way she lights up when she talks about something she believes in. But I also watch the Romero out of the corner of my eye, my body tight with the knowledge that dinner in Manhattan just turned into something else entirely. Something with stakes. Something I'll have to tell Lucien about and our brothers.

Somewhere near the kitchen doors, a server drops a fork, the sharp clink cutting briefly through the soft murmur of the dining room.

And I don't know yet whether Dallen is going to be the safest thing I've ever wanted—or the most dangerous.

EIGHT

DALLEN

"So that's why I'm a lawyer and a very good one. Now," I stop talking about myself, wanting to know more about this mysterious man whom I can't stop thinking about. "Tell me what you do?"

"I'm in real estate." His eyes dart yet again to something behind me. I lean back in my chair, pretending to adjust my seat before I turn to look at what's capturing his attention. Nothing at the bar or the restaurant looks out of place. There are people sitting at the bar drinking and talking, no doubt waiting for their tables to be ready, and those already dining.

What the hell is distracting him?

Maybe he isn't as interested in me as I think he is.

I don't say anything, merely watch him watch something else, and don't ask anything more. I pick up my wine and finish it. Maybe I should leave. Maybe one-night stands that start off hot and heavy are as baseless as I fear they are.

Maybe he isn't one of the nice guys.

Maybe there isn't anything here except chemistry, because whether he's ignoring me or not, distracted for some unknown reason, he's hot as hell. And I still can't get the orgasm he gave me—the first not brought on by myself—out of my head.

Still, that's no basis to keep seeing someone. To date them just because they're good in bed will never work out.

"Have you sold much?" I ask, attempting one last time to get his attention back.

I wait, and perhaps it's the silence, the long stretch between our conversation, that makes his attention finally snap back to me.

"I'm sorry. I thought I saw someone I knew." He adjusts his tie and sips his wine. He glances at my glass, notes it's empty, and reaches for the bottle to refill it without asking.

I don't say anything. He seems the kind of guy who's used to getting his way without asking, and I would like another glass if I'm going to stay. Although that's still to be determined.

"I work for my family's business and purchase the real estate that I believe may be a good investment for us, both here in the US and overseas."

"Oh wow, that sounds more exciting than my job. Although I do travel a lot. I often fly out to London or Paris, as we have firms in both locations."

He studies me intensely, and I feel my skin prickle with awareness. That delicious warmth settles in the pit of my stomach, and there it is again—that chemistry that wraps around us like a piece of string.

Isn't that a thing? The red-string theory? Pretty sure it is...

Our main course, roasted duck with an orange-ginger glaze, is placed before us. The scent of the orange teases my senses, and I understand completely why there is such a waitlist to come dine here.

"This smells delicious. I can't wait to devour it."

Stephen growls as he picks up his fork and knife. "I couldn't agree more."

Our eyes meet across the table, and I know to my very marshmallowy core he doesn't mean the food, but me. Devour? Does he want to eat me that badly?

I bite my lip, unable to stop the memory of the last time he went down on me. My attention moves to his mouth as he chews his food. He has a very clever tongue, and he obviously enjoys women, or he wouldn't do something so intimate to them.

Lucky for me, I guess.

Without a word, he moves to sit beside me, shifting his plate and glassware without raising an eyebrow elsewhere in the restaurant. He's so close to me now. I can feel his heat and smell his cologne.

A faint clink of cutlery from nearby tables blends with a low hum of conversation.

I breathe deep. Damn, he smells good.

I start as his hand slips onto my thigh, squeezing my leg. I meet his gaze, and I can see nothing but determination burning in his brown eyes.

I look around, hoping the long, white tablecloth will hide anything Stephen has in store for me. Having thought of nothing else but his hands on me the last half hour, even with his distraction, all I want is for him to touch me. Feeling far bolder than I should, I reach below the table and slip my hand on top of his. His are large, strong, and a little coarse. Hands that don't seem to suit the occupation he holds.

I move his hand upward, toward my weeping sex that wants nothing but to be touched, even here in the middle of this beautiful restaurant.

His eyes darken with hunger. I relish the sight of him looking at me in this way. Like I'm the only person in the world, the only person he desires.

"Naughty girl."

His deep, gravelly voice whispered against my ear does things to me no one else ever has. Makes me want to be what he wants, what he'd like. What I'd like to be. "Only when around you," I admit, not sure if I should be so vulnerable so soon into knowing this man, but we've already done more than most. I can't see what the harm is.

He leans close and kisses my neck. It's electric. I feel his warm mouth as if it's kissing all over my body, and I'm helpless to stop him. I ache for him, want him with a need that's fierce and strange, but wonderful, too.

"You smell so good," he whispers. His hand presses against my sex. With nimble ease, he works his hand under my panties. We lock eyes, and he's all wickedness. I love it. I want him to touch me, make me feel as good as I know he can.

"And wet. You want me, Dallen?"

I swallow, nodding. I do want him, but I fear if I speak right at this moment, others in the restaurant will hear—hear the need in my voice that may give away what Stephen is doing to me under the tablecloth.

He glides one finger into my sex, and I clasp the table, spreading my legs and hoping no one can see. I am wet, so embarrassingly so that I doubt I'll ever live down the shame, but I don't push him away.

He fucks me with his hand before everyone in the restaurant and I'm powerless to stop him. I don't want to stop him. I want more. Thoughts of pushing him back in his chair, straddling his legs, and guiding him into me bombard my mind. Of him picking me up, thrusting everything on the table to the floor, and eating me for his dinner instead of the meal we've come out for.

"Dallen? Is that you?"

The sound of my mother's voice douses my desire instantly.

Stephen pulls back as if nothing untoward is happening and picks up his wine just as my mother walks over from near the door with several of her friends. Out for dinner themselves, no doubt to gossip and speak down on those who are unfortunate enough not to be as wealthy as they are.

"Mother." I smile, although my body mourns the touch of Stephen. My mother glances at my date, and I see the moment she disapproves of my choice. Stephen stills beside me, and I know he's discerning her dissatisfaction also.

"I didn't know you had a date this evening, darling," she says, watching Stephen.

"Ah, yes, surprising, I know..." I clear my throat. "Mother, this is Stephen. Stephen, this is my mother, Susan."

"A pleasure," he states and says nothing else.

My mother's lips turn down in distaste as her gaze lingers on the tattoos on Stephen's hands.

"Hmm, likewise," she responds, her tone meaning

the opposite. "Well, dear, I hope you have a lovely evening. Do ring me tomorrow. We should do lunch."

I nod, smiling at her friends who are watching the exchange. "Yes, of course." She moves on when a waiter notifies them their table is ready, and I take a deep, relieved breath that she's gone.

"I didn't put you down for a mummy's girl. Mother?"

I don't know if I like being put in such a box, and to be fair, I've never really thought about what I call my parents as sounding odd to others. "Call it instinct, but I believe my mother will not approve of me calling her 'Mom.' My father, however, is happy to be called 'Dad.'" He doesn't say anything, and I feel the need to explain. "She's from a wealthy founding family of New York. The term is common practice on her side of the family. Formal speech is the only way they know how to communicate."

He doesn't respond, merely sips his wine and finishes another glass. I wonder if it's a turnoff hearing a woman calling their parent such a formal form of address. "Does it matter what I call my parents? You disapprove?"

"Your mother dislikes me, that is clear. It makes me wonder if this is worth pursuing if you're the type of daughter who'll do whatever the parent thinks best. I'm not ever going to be what's best for you, no matter how much you may want me to be. I'm not an untat-tooed banker from a good family with aristocratic roots."

I frown, fighting not to allow my rage to trigger me into a fiery exchange with Stephen. "You're being very judgmental, considering you barely know me or my relationship with my parents." Even if what he states is true up to a point, what does it matter that I obey rules? Of course, I rely on my parents and their advice. They are my only family after losing Daniel.

"It's clear you're a good girl until I fuck you in my car and take your virginity. Is this just sex for you? Not that I have an issue scratching your itch—you're hot as fuck—but I won't change to please anyone, and it's pointless if that's your intention."

His bluntness steals my breath, and I look around, hoping no one hears us. I wave over a waiter, who comes immediately, and without waiting, I reach into my purse and hand him my card. "Please put the meal on me, thank you."

Stephen leans back in his chair, and I can feel him staring at me. "You're leaving?"

I scoff. "I'm certainly not staying." I pick up my wine, hoping my hands don't shake. He is right in a lot of ways. I am naïve and perhaps lean on my parents too much, care too much about what they think. But to have that opinion shoved in my face isn't what I want to hear—not five minutes after he's been fingering me at the table.

I'm a lawyer. Of course, I'm not a criminal or a woman who changes partners as often as her panties. I've always struggled to put myself out there in an intimate way. He's the first man I want, really desire, and to feel ridiculed isn't what I expect after such a lovely meal together.

Hurt coils inside me, and I blink, fighting the tears that threaten.

The waiter returns, handing my card back. "Thank you," I say before starting to collect my things. "It was nice meeting you, Stephen. A shame you think the way you do. We may have suited, no matter our differences in upbringing."

I feel his gaze—hot and a little unhinged—on me as I pick up my bag. I push back my chair and start for the door. I hear his chair scrape, and before I reach the door, his arm is on the small of my back, pressing me in the direction he wants.

Not where I was heading.

Home.

NINE

STEPHEN

I SHOULDN'T PUSH DALLEN OR PRACTICALLY insult her mother on our first date, but fuck that judgmental bitch. And I know, just by looking at Dallen's mother's face, that she is just that. A woman who will not approve and will probably have a stroke if she learns who my family is.

There is no point to us. Even so, the sight of her leaving—of casting me aside—isn't something I can stomach. Maybe I just can't stand being abandoned again, or maybe pride stings sharper than truth. Panic, sharp and foreign, grips my chest. I'm not the kind of man to panic over a woman walking away.

What on earth is wrong with me?

I catch up to her at the door, the cold wind cutting between us like a blade as we exit the restaurant. A gust sweeps down the street, rattling the metal chairs stacked outside, the city's noise momentarily muffled beneath the rush of air.

"Dallen, wait."

She doesn't. Doesn't even look back. Her shoulders stiffen, her pace quickens, and something ugly twists inside me. I reach out, catching her arm—not hard, just enough to stop her.

She spins on me instantly. "Let go."

I do. Immediately. But I don't move back. "You're running."

"I'm walking," she snapped. "Away from you."

"And that's any different?" I ask. "Just throwing in the towel because I said one thing you didn't like?"

"It wasn't one thing," she hisses. "You insulted my mother, how I am with my family. You insulted me."

"I stated a fact."

Her eyes flash fire. "No. You judged me because you were pissed off that my mother didn't fawn over you the moment you met."

I rake a hand through my hair, frustration simmering beneath my skin. "Who wouldn't judge anyone who looked at another person like they were dirt? Like I wasn't good enough to breathe your air." And maybe I don't deserve to breathe her air. I should let this go, here and now. I've allowed things in my family to be okay—things others would have a hard time processing. Even if I want to drag Dallen into that, I shouldn't. She's a lawyer, for crying out loud.

"She didn't say anything—"

"She didn't have to," I bite out. "Her face said enough."

Dallen shakes her head, anger thinning her voice. "You don't even know her. You don't know me. But you've already decided I'm...what? A mummy-and-daddy's girl who does whatever they tell me?"

Her words hit with the same weight as a slap. I exhale, slow and long. "If the shoe fits." The moment the words slip from my lips, I regret them. They're too sharp, too blunt, too fucking revealing of my own insecurities.

I'm not good enough for her. I know that, but it doesn't mean I want *her* to realize that, too.

Her jaw drops. "Wow. You really think that lowly of me? That I'm some...obedient little good girl who just nods at whatever my parents want?"

"Isn't that what you've been doing your whole life?" I challenge. "They say jump, you ask how high. One chance meeting with your mother just now, and I know that's the relationship you have with them. They push you toward some perfect man, and you entertain the idea. They say I'm wrong for you, you run."

She steps close, fury radiating off her. She looks so fucking beautiful when mad—so goddamn sexy. I want to reach for her, push her up against the parked car beside us, and show her what she does to me. Instead, I fist my hands at my sides and force myself to calm the hell down.

"I didn't run because of them. I ran because of you. Because you were being an ass."

"I was being honest."

"You were being a spiteful bastard, and I don't need that in my life."

I clench my jaw. Fuck. "Sometimes the truth hurts."

Her eyes darken, hurt threading through the anger. Guilt digs claws beneath my ribs. But I power through it because the alternative—being vulnerable—is worse.

She folds her arms across her chest. "So that's what you think I am? That I have no mind of my own? That I'm weak?"

"No," I say, a bit too quickly. "That's not—"

"Yes," she cuts in. "You do. You don't think I can choose for myself."

"Then prove me wrong," I challenge before I can stop myself. "Stay. Don't run because your mother frowned at me, and I was offended."

"There it is." She barks a humorless laugh. "You think she controls me, Stephen. But I'm a grown woman who can choose what I do with my life, no matter what you think after one interaction."

"With a mother who still treats you like you're fourteen."

"And you think you get to judge that?"

"I think," I say carefully, fury and fear warring within me, "that I don't want to be with someone who lets her parents dictate her life." I can't be with someone like that. I need someone on my side, even if that side is sometimes the wrong one. Whoever I end up with has to have my back as much as I would have theirs.

Her mouth tightens. "Then maybe you shouldn't be with me at all."

The words land like a punch. I don't flinch—but I feel every ounce of it. "Is that what you want?" I ask, voice low.

Her lips part. She looks away, breathing hard.

"That's what I thought," I murmur, hating that she is so agreeable even if she can't admit it.

She snaps back. "That is *not* what you thought. You think I'm scared of upsetting them. You think I'm...obedient." Her eyes narrow on me. "I'm not."

"No?" I step closer, crowding her without touching. "Then why are you so defensive about it?"

"Because you're wrong."

"Then show me," I repeat, wanting her to go against her better judgment—her mother's judgment—and choose me, here and now.

Her breath catches, and my pulse jolts. Maybe I pushed too hard. But every part of me rebels at the idea of her walking away.

I drag a hand down my face. "Dallen, look... I don't think you're weak. Or that you're your mother's puppet. I just—" I exhale. "I don't know how any of this works if your family hates me on sight." They will hate me enough once they know my name and those who make up my family.

"My family doesn't—"

"Your mother does." I let out a dry laugh. "And she hasn't even Googled me yet."

Dallen's spine straightens. "What would she find if she Googled you? What is your name. Your full name?"

The wind whips between us, tugging at her hair, but neither of us moves. A taxi horn blares somewhere behind us, the city pressing in as if eavesdropping on a fight it has heard a thousand times before.

"I'm Stephen Moretti and I'm pretty sure if she looked me up, there's nothing she'd approve of."

She stares up at me, eyes a storm. "I don't care what my mother thinks. I make up my own mind with regard to the men I date."

"Liar."

Her chin jerks up. "Fine. I care, but not enough to let her ruin something I want."

My heart kicks hard. "You want this?" I ask, softer now, the anger dissipating like smoke. "Because there's no turning back if you do. I want in. I want you, and I won't care if both your parents hate me on sight. I'll not let them or anyone take you if I commit."

She hesitates—but only for a second. "I thought I wanted you." She pauses. "Well, I did until you pissed me off."

Something inside my chest eases, just a fraction. "Come with me."

"Where?"

"To my car," I say. "Because we're not debating this on a sidewalk while half of Manhattan passes by."

Her lips part—ready to argue again—but I reach for her hand, not pulling, just offering. After a beat, she takes it, doesn't speak as we walk to the car. The tension is still thick, but different now—coiled, electric, the kind that hums beneath the skin. Something that always happens the moment we touch.

I open the passenger door. She slides in without meeting my eyes. I round to the driver's side and climb in, shutting the door.

Silence greets me.

Her chest rises and falls—fast, sharp. I can feel her anger. Her emotions war in the confined space. My hands curl around the steering wheel. I fight the urge to reach for her before she finally turns in her seat, facing me.

Then she does something I don't expect. She climbs over the center console—swinging one leg across mine, then the other until she's straddling me. Her dress rides up. Her breath fans my face. Her anger hasn't vanished—no, it vibrates between us, thrumming like a live wire—but the way she looks at me makes everything inside me go still.

"Does this look like someone who does what she's told?" she whispers, fire in her voice, in her eyes, in every inch of her body pressed to mine.

I swallow hard. "Not even close," I manage to mumble, completely thrown off guard.

I press the door lock, glad for the tinted windows. Her hands frame my jaw—not gentle, not soft, but firm, commanding.

She's so fucking hot.

"And does this look like someone who runs away because her mother frowns at you?"

"No," I rasped. "It looks like someone who's about to ruin me."

A faint, wicked smile touches her lips. "Good." She leans in, close enough that her breath brushes my mouth—but doesn't kiss me. Not yet. She holds the tension there, coiling it, daring me.

Daring us.

I'll take that dare and double it.

I take her lips in a kiss that is wild and unhinged. Her tongue tangles with mine. When she pulls back, I nip her lip, trying to coax her back to kiss me again. I want her, my cock hard, erect, weeping to sheath itself in her hot heat.

"Fuck me," I order her.

She reaches between us and works the button and zipper of my pants, opening them. I push into her palm, and she strokes me harder still. My eyes roll to the back of my head, and I lean against the headrest, fighting the urge to take over, to rip her panties in half and off her body and thrust myself into her.

I've never wanted to fuck someone so hard in my life as I do right at this moment. I want to punish her for flaunting the life she enjoyed while I went without, to make her feel what I felt. To mark her as mine and no one else's—certainly not her snobbish parents.

I'm breathless, my head spinning. Who is this woman who's charmed her way under my skin?

I can't get enough of her.

She pulls her panties to the side and slips down onto my cock. I groan. She's so wet, a perfect fit. Her cunt wraps around my dick like a glove, pulling it, teasing it. I'm hard as hell, and I thrust into her, clasping her hips, no longer able to stop the need that pulsates through me.

"Oh yeah, Stephen. Fuck me."

A shiver runs over my body at her words, her plea. I won't disappoint. I thrust up, relishing the sound of her gasp as I take her deep. My large cock stretches her sweet, tight pussy.

I'm wrong. She isn't a good girl at all. Not here with me. Not like this. She is a Siren, and I can't ignore her call.

Sweat beads our skin. I can smell our sex, her hot, wet cunt. My mouth waters. I'm going to eat her again. I'm going to hold her down, force her to orgasm, to climax on my face, and relish every second of it.

Her body shakes, and I kiss her hard and deep as her orgasm rips through her. Her body convulses around my cock, dragging me into my own release. I come hard, emptying myself into her, deep and sure.

I don't care about the consequences—an oddity for me and one I'll think upon later. But right now, nothing seems righter.

"Dallen..." I can't form more words. My body spent, drained, left expended and empty, satisfied and content.

"Take back what you said," she says, meeting my gaze, her face a picture of satisfaction. "Apologize, or this ends now."

I kiss her, claim her mouth again, before leaning back and watching her a moment. Should I deny her request? Should I argue the point and see if she'll fuck me into submission again? Nothing is hotter than when a woman takes control, and considering I'm a control freak and like things done my way, that too is new for me.

"I take it back. You're not a good girl," I say. "I'm sorry."

A small, wicked yet satisfied smile twists her mouth. "I'm good most of the time, except when I'm around you, then I lose all my inhibitions. But don't call me out on it again, or this will end."

End? Hell no.

We're just beginning.

TEN

DALLEN

I RETURN HOME TO MY APARTMENT, AND A VOICE message from my mother comes through on my phone. I take a deep breath, already knowing it'll be an invitation to lunch or another dinner mid-week after she's seen me with the mystery man she didn't like.

Stephen is right about that, at least. My mother is never backward in coming forward, and if she doesn't like you, you know it.

I press play on the message and—just as I assumed —a lunch date, tomorrow.

Wow, she must really be worried. In her mind, I've thrown my life away with the tattooed stranger—he looks far rougher on the outside than he is.

I like him, even though tonight he annoyed me by calling me a good girl. I sigh and throw my bag onto the kitchen bench, and go pick up Puss Puss, kissing her pretty little face and forcing affection on her that she's probably not entirely enjoying.

Maybe he is right about me. I've always been a rule-follower, trying to do the right thing. Does that make me boring?

Is he calling me boring?

After I fucked him in his car—seeing shock and desire twist his features—I doubt he'll call me boring again soon.

Or at least he better not, or he can disappear as quickly as he appeared.

I grin, remembering my boldness. My body warms and tingles with the thought of doing more. Of doing him again.

Gah, I need to get a grip. I have work tomorrow.

I sleep restlessly that night, despite having one of my best orgasms. Granted, there haven't been many courtesy of men, but still, sleep eludes me.

I shower and dress in a comfortable pair of black trousers and a white shirt, then pull on a dark navy jacket. I respond to my mother via text, telling her I can spare a quick hour for lunch at my work's cafeteria if she's in the area, and what time that is, before heading off to work.

Upon arriving at the office, I barely have time to sit down before my work phone rings.

"Dallen speaking."

"Dallen, it's George. Come to the conference room. We have a new client who's asked for you personally," he instructs.

"Sure, I'll be right in," I reply. I set my bag down, grab my phone and laptop, and head into the conference room. I greet several colleagues already in the office with a good morning before knocking and entering the room.

I smile as I take in who's seated at the table. I look to the gentleman's left and see another, one who I'm sure I haven't met before but looks familiar.

Brothers or cousins, perhaps. They have to be.

"Dallen, this is Elio and Alex Romero. They're looking for new representation for their business interests, real estate, and financial investments, and asked for you. Your reputation precedes you, it seems."

I set down my laptop and reach out to shake both men's hands. I take my seat. "Of course, it's a pleasure to meet you both." I open my laptop and prepare a work form to take notes and see what they're specifically looking for. "If you could let me know what you're after, go through your assets and business plans, we can get started."

The meeting progresses well, but the niggling realization that Alex Romero looks familiar to me doesn't dissipate; I still can't place him. He's also the less talkative of the two, but far more intense, like he's trying to work me out as much as I'm evaluating him.

If I'm to be their lawyer—and I do my job well—that's all he needs to know about me.

"Our cousin passed last year, and we're looking to ensure the assets that he left to the family are properly allocated and protected. He was murdered, you see, and we're not used to handling such large quantities of investments that he acquired during his life," Elio says.

I look down at my notes, needing to remember the deceased gentleman's name. "Matteo Romero was a cousin of yours, is that correct?"

"Yes, that's correct. He was murdered almost a year ago, and we've recently been notified of some real estate he has shares in that we believe is linked to his downfall. We would like to sell the shares of the building, and we're hoping you'll also be able to handle those contracts, among other legalities that may arise, of course," Elio continues.

"Of course, I can help with that," I say. "Do you have the contract for his shares in the building? I want to review it to see who the other investors are and identify potential contacts who might be willing to buy your shares at an agreed market value."

Elio Romero slides some paperwork over to me, and I pick it up, looking through it. The name Stephen

Moretti jumps out at me, and I fight to hide my surprise.

That can't be the Stephen that I was with but a few hours ago? No. This is a coincidence.

I look up and find Alex staring at me intently as if he's waiting for me to say something. "I'll go over the contracts, look into what the shares are worth, and reach out to the other parties. I should have a response for you all by next week. Shall we meet back here next Monday? My assistant will get back to you regarding a time," I say.

"Sounds good, Miss Byrne," Elio says, standing. "Thank you for taking us on. We look forward to doing business with you."

"My pleasure," I reply, standing. They come around the desk, shake my hand, before moving toward the door. Alex looks back before he exits, and I school my features to professional indifference, but the moment they leave, I breathe a sigh of relief.

That was intense. I'm not sure why Alex Romero rattles me. I sit and review the contract, noting Stephen's name with Lucien Moretti and Moretti Global.

I open a new tab on my laptop, search for Moretti Global, and see numerous news articles about the family. The family had been heavily involved in mafia-style business dealings in the past.

I frown. Surely that can't be right. Stephen works in real estate.

I do a search on him, and hundreds of deals come up, some worth millions upon millions of dollars, but always alongside those searches is the mention of their father, Leo Moretti. The many deaths linked to him. His obscene alleged body count before he, too, found his end in a dark New York alleyway.

I can't reconcile the man I've met with the one who seems to be from this family, and yet, maybe I've been naïve.

No. I dismiss the idea immediately. Just because someone is tattooed, dark, and mysterious does not mean they're part of the New York underworld. Stephen is a real estate broker; he says so himself, that he looks after all his family's portfolio.

My stomach churns, and I close my laptop, leaving the room and heading back to my desk. I sit and stare out the window for several minutes. I don't know what to do with this information, if it's true.

I'm a lawyer. My father's the Chief of Police. What if the man I'm seeing—the one I've slept with—is crooked? I have to end it before it begins.

I hate the idea of such an outcome, but what choice do I have? I don't have a choice.

I can't date someone who could bring my world tumbling down.

ELEVEN

STEPHEN

THE CHARITY EVENT COMES AROUND QUICKER than I think. I haven't seen Dallen for several days. In fact, a few of my messages have been ignored, left unread, or replied to with one-word answers.

What the fuck is going on?

I plan to ask her to come with me. I don't know if she'll care about who I am or my family name when she Googles me.

Maybe it's wishful thinking she knows who I am and the family I hail from, and she's too polite to dump my ass the old-fashioned way...in person.

I pull on my evening jacket and roll my shoulders, adjusting the fit to be more comfortable. I stare at myself in the mirror, my suit barely concealing the tatts that are over my hands that go all the way up my arms. A few are visible where my tie sits. I look good enough for a charity event, one my family is hosting and donating to along with everyone else in this city who has money.

A knock sounds on my door, and I turn to find my housekeeper, an older woman, standing on the threshold of the room. "Your car is here, Mr. Moretti."

"Thank you, May, and remember what I said. No more Mr. Moretti, you can call me Stephen."

She smiles and doesn't respond, merely walks back to where she rules this house, the kitchen, where she cooks some of the best meals I've ever had in my life. She's the best investment I've ever made, and although I bring in millions of dollars to the family business through real estate, having someone cook delicious, wholesome, healthy meals is one of life's blessings.

A blessing that was denied to my brothers and me as kids. Our father couldn't have given a shit if we ate or died.

I push the memory down and start for the elevator. "Thanks again, May. I'll see you tomorrow after lunch."

"Have a good evening, Mr. Moretti."

I sigh, laughing to myself that no matter how much I try, I can't break her into calling me by my given name. I ride the elevator down to the foyer and start for the car where my driver waits. The distance to the Met is short from where I live, and skipping the red carpet, I enter the gala and start to interact with the invited guests.

I play the part my brother Lucien has taught us all, complimenting, teasing, and boasting as good as anyone else who is present, all in the hopes that those here tonight will open their check books and be generous.

Most are generous; some are harder to convince.

I enter the dining room, where the night's auction will take place, and look for where I'll be seated. I read the place setting board and narrow my eyes. The Chief of Police. I purse my lips and turn to take in the room. At least sitting next to law and order should make the night interesting.

I spy Elio and Alex Romero, and any enjoyment I was pretending to have regarding the night vanishes. What the hell are they doing here?

I turn and look for Lucien, spying him near the bar and thankfully alone. Briar doesn't need to know the relatives of her slain ex-husband are here, not before she sees them for herself.

"Lucien, did you invite the Romeros?" The question is out before I'm three feet from him.

Lucien hands me a glass of bourbon and takes a sip of his drink. "Yes, I thought it would look less obvious I offed their cousin if they were invited. Not to mention they do have money, maybe not as much as they used to, but it would have looked strange, I thought, if I hadn't extended the invitation."

"It would have looked perfectly fine. There isn't any love lost between our families, hasn't been for many years, even before Briar."

"She knows they're here and is well guarded and will stay clear of them, but she knows what she has to do to keep what we have safe. So if she can play that role this evening, so can you." My brother pats my chest before giving my face a light slap. "Okay, brother?"

"I'd prefer to off them myself than have to see them here."

"We'll try not to, but I hear they've hired a new law firm. Redwood & Tully from all accounts. Matteo's cousins have inherited his assets, and they want the law firm to look into their whereabouts and whether they can do anything with them. I hear Matteo had more real estate than I realized. We may be able to do a deal with these two goons; they don't appear as bright as Matteo, not that he was ever overly intelligent either."

I scoff and see our head of security and cousin Anthony walking around the room with Briar as she speaks to guests. My attention moves over those who are already in the dining room. My heart slams into my chest at the sight of Dallen, with her delightful mother at her side, and I'm assuming the tall, middle-aged gentleman behind them to be her father.

"Ah, yes, the Chief of Police is here. I put him at your table. I thought you'd find the night more interesting with him as a table guest."

Lucien's laugh grates on my nerves, and I seriously consider for a moment popping him one on the jaw. "Yeah, sure." I narrow my eyes on the three of them. "Is that their daughter?" Dallen can't be the Chief of Police's daughter.

"Yes, Dallen Byrne..." Lucien claps me on the shoulder, and I still. "Hey, isn't that the redhead from the club the other night? The one you left with?"

I nod, downing the last of my bourbon. "Yeah. Same one." Shit.

"Well, your night just got even more enjoyable. Behave yourself," Lucien says, before sauntering off.

I don't move, unable to shift my weight forward.

The room's noise dulls to a distant hum. It is like I've been pushed underwater. All I can see is her. Dallen. Silver dress skimming her curves. Red, luscious hair twisted up to show off that soft throat I've kissed. Her hand looped through her mother's arm. Her smile tight, brittle. The man behind them—tall, graying, built like he used to be a linebacker—watches the room with a cop's discernment.

Chief of fucking Police.

Of course he is. She's a damn lawyer; why wouldn't he also be in law enforcement?

Heat creeps up the back of my neck, a charred flavor settles on my tongue that tastes a hell of a lot like insult. I drag in a breath, rolling my shoulders back, setting my face into that calm, bored expression that gets me through board meetings and murder cleanups alike.

She didn't tell me he's the Chief of Police.

I'm a Moretti.

That won't suit, no matter how you try to force them to. It would be like two magnets flipped over, forever moving around each other but never coming together.

I let the thoughts settle, line themselves up. It doesn't change what happened in the car. It doesn't change how her nails dug into my shoulders, or the way she whispered my name like a prayer and a curse combined when she climaxed on my cock. It doesn't change that, when I wake up, she's the first thing I think of.

I take one step, then another, crossing the room.

A few heads turn. They always do. People see my face, they see the tux, the watch that costs more than most cars, and they decide I'm important or dangerous or both. And they're right.

Dallen looks up at that moment, like she can feel

me coming. Her eyes go wide. The color drains from her cheeks so fast I almost think she's going to faint. Her gaze flicks from me to Lucien across the room, to the huge Moretti crest on the sponsor backdrop near the stage, and back to me.

There it is. Recognition. Not Stephen-who-made-her-come-in-the-backseat-of-his-car. Stephen Moretti. At least I know she's now Googled me. Maybe I won't have to explain myself or my family's past after all. As a lawyer, I think she knows more about me than I do.

My stomach knots as her features harden the closer I move toward her. Dallen's fingers tighten on her mother's arm before she, too, follows her daughter's line of sight, and her lips thin when she sees me. She's already met me once, with a less-than-favorable response, like I smell wrong.

Rotten maybe.

Now her eyes are ice.

Obviously, I won't be winning Dallen's mother over.

I don't slow down because I need to face this directly. I'm not the one who hides; if there's fallout, I want to deal with it head-on. They came into my world, not the other way around. "Dallen," I say when I'm close enough. Her name fits in my mouth too easily. It shouldn't.

She startles like I've touched her, even though I'm

still a step away. "Mr. Moretti." Her voice is barely above a whisper. "Good evening."

I reach for her hand automatically, fingers lifting toward her elbow, wanting to feel her, to anchor this mess with something real. I want that little spark I always get when my skin brushes hers, the one I've been thinking about for days.

She flinches.

Actually flinches.

Her hand jerks out of my reach so fast she might as well have slapped me. My hand hangs there—suspended between us. Empty, stupid, exposed.

For a second, everything inside me goes still.

Right. Message received.

I let my hand fall back to my side, slow, controlled, like I meant to do it that way. I force myself to mask the humiliation—this isn't unfamiliar. I remind myself it's survival, not pride, that keeps me composed.

Her mother steps half a pace closer to Dallen, like she's shielding her from me. Like I'm the threat here. Perhaps she's more clever than I gave her credit for.

"Darling," the Chief says, his voice carrying that measured authority you hear on press conferences and crime documentaries. "Aren't you going to introduce us to your friend?"

Friend?

If I weren't the one bleeding internally, I'd laugh.

Dallen swallows, straightens, and forces a smile that doesn't reach her eyes. "Yes. Of course." Her fingers twist in the fabric of her clutch so hard her knuckles turn white. "Mother, Dad...this is Stephen Moretti, one of our hosts this evening." She pauses. "Mr. Moretti, these are my parents, Susan and Thomas Byrne."

The way she leaves it there—all formal like I'm not someone who she's kind of seeing—lands like a king hit.

I'm not some nameless nobody she picked up at a bar, nothing but the host for the evening. I might be the devil in every cop's bedtime story, but I built half the skyline these people are drinking under tonight. I've clawed my way out of my father's mess and bled for every inch of legitimacy we have.

I'm not hiding who the fuck I am.

I give her a small, cool smile, then turn to her parents. I extend my hand to the Chief. "It's an honor to meet you, Chief Byrne. Thank you for coming tonight and for your service to our great city."

His eyes narrow, a flicker of recognition sparking there. As the Chief of Police, of course he knows who my family is. Ordinarily, I doubt he'd care, so long as we kept ourselves clean, but my knowing his daughter, dating her possibly, that was something else altogether.

He doesn't move to shake my hand, leaves me out there, hanging again. People nearby could be watching.

I don't look to check. I just keep my hand steady, my jaw relaxed, like I'm not timing each heartbeat he makes me wait, but I won't wait forever.

Finally, he takes it.

His grip is firm. Not crushing, but deliberate. Testing. I meet his gaze and squeeze back just as hard, no more, no less. I've shaken hands with men who've ordered hits and priests who've given last rites. A handshake can tell you a lot about a man.

This one says: I know exactly what you are, and I'm not impressed.

"Mr. Moretti," he says, voice flat. "I've heard your name."

Not "nice to meet you." Not even a fake thank-you for the charity donations we've made to his own department's youth programs. Just that he's heard of my name. "I get that a lot," I reply lightly. "Hopefully for the right reasons these days."

One of his brows lifts, the smallest twitch of disdain. "That depends on who you ask."

I see Dallen tense, like a wire pulled too tight. Her hand hovers near her father's arm, as if she's not sure if she should touch him or me or neither. Her mother is watching me like I'm something she's stepped in.

I turn to her because I was raised with manners, even if they were carved into me by a violent man.

"Mrs. Byrne," I say with a nod. "Good to see you again."

"We've met?" Her tone is frosted glass.

"When I was out to dinner several days ago with Dallen," I remind her. "You were dining with friends." I let a hint of amusement curve my lips.

Recognition flickers in her eyes, followed immediately by annoyance that she's spoken to me at all. "Ah. Yes." She gives me her hand like it's costing her something, fingers limp, as if actual contact might infect her.

I take it briefly and let go. If she wants distance, I can give her miles.

The awkwardness stretches like gum between us, sticky and unbreakable.

"How do you know our daughter?" the Chief asks then, cutting straight through the bullshit. He looks at Dallen when he speaks, but the question is aimed at me. A cross-examination.

My heart gives one hard thud. That's the thing about men like him, they don't waste time.

Dallen beats me to it. "We...met on a night out," she says quickly, that bright fake smile plastered on again. She doesn't look at me, and that hurts more than I want to admit. "Remember when I told you I got a ride home. It is Mr. Moretti who was kind enough to give me one. Our meeting is totally by chance."

It is by chance, but I saw her in the club and moved

to the bar to be near her, to see if she was there with anyone. But the benign, cold way in which she terms our first meeting, well, that won't do at all. I'll be reminding her later that I did a lot more than just give her a ride home. She rode me, if memory serves me right.

The Chief turns his full attention on me, weighing every inch, every line of my expensive suit. "Moretti Global," he repeats slowly. "Quite the operation."

"We try," I say. "Shipping, construction, and real estate. A few other ventures. You've got a couple of our developments on your beat, I imagine. The community center on Forty-Second, the youth complex in Queens—"

"Funded by blood money," Mrs. Byrne murmurs under her breath. It's barely audible, but I catch it. Of course I do.

Heat flashes under my skin, hot and savage. I keep my smile, but it tightens at the edges. A part of me wants to lean in and ask her if she prefers her daughter fucking a broke accountant instead. Another part wants to walk away before I say something that will have Lucien dragging me off the front page of tomorrow's papers.

Instead, I let the anger settle, cold and heavy. I'm used to this. To be the villain in every room I walk into.

But this is different. Because they don't just hate a

name. They hate me. And she's standing there, my girl who kissed me like I am the only man she's ever wanted, letting them.

Fine.

If they want a villain, I can oblige.

"You're welcome to come see the books anytime, Mrs. Byrne," I say, voice silky. "We've been audited more than most Fortune 500 companies. Everything above board. That's the beauty of going legitimate. People can dig all they like and find nothing but tax returns and building permits."

The Chief studies me with that cop stare that feels like an internal examination. "Some stains don't wash off, Mr. Moretti. No matter how many buildings you put your name on."

My jaw ticks. "Some stains built this city," I shoot back softly. "At least we're using ours to give something back, not merely pretending to help at yearly held charities."

There's a tiny, almost invisible wince from Dallen. She finally looks at me, properly, and the sheen of confusion and hurt in her eyes slices straight through my armor.

You could have told me, I want to say. *About your father. About who you are. You could have given me a chance to tell you who I am, too.*

Instead, I tip my head slightly, eyes never leaving

the Chief's. "We're glad you're here tonight," I say. "Your presence means something to the donors, to the press, and to the kids these programs help. Optics matter, don't they?"

He knows what I'm doing. We both do. If he walks out now, he looks petty. Political. Like a man with a personal vendetta instead of a public servant. And he can't afford that.

So he gives me a smile with no warmth. "I'm here for the cause," he says. "Not the company."

"Of course." I let the lie sit there. "I hope you enjoy the evening."

The mother gives a brittle laugh. "We'll do our best."

Lucien's voice booms from across the room as he calls everyone to take their seats, the lights dimming a fraction. The usual shuffle and murmur follow as people start drifting toward their tables.

"You're at my table," I tell them, because if I'm going to be judged, I want front-row seats. "What a jolly night this will be." Sarcasm laces my words. I hold Dallen's gaze for one last heartbeat. There's so much I want to say in that look. *Don't let them decide who I am for you. Don't run. Don't you dare pretend what happened between us was nothing.*

She looks away first.

The cold, hard thing inside me snaps into place.

All right, sweetheart. If this is how your family wants to play it, I can play.

They think I'm not good enough? They think a Moretti is something you scrape off your shoe? Fine. I'll show them exactly what happens when you look down on a man who's spent his whole life crawling out of the gutter they shoved him in.

I turn away, walking back toward our table, my stride easy, unhurried. People nod, smile, call my name, and I let the charm slide back into place like a well-tailored coat.

But under it, something sharp and possessive has lodged deep.

They don't know it yet, but the more they push her away from me, the more they make it impossible for me to let her go. I don't lose. Not business deals. Not real estate. And definitely not the woman who finally makes me want more than the next deal, the next night, the next anonymous fuck.

If the Chief of Police and his ice-queen wife want to keep their perfect daughter away from the big, bad Moretti? I'm going to enjoy proving them wrong.

TWELVE

DALLEN

I CAN BARELY SWALLOW AS WE TAKE OUR SEATS AT the round table. The chatter in the room swells around us while my pulse pounds, as if trying to punch its way out of my throat. A woman—Lucien Morettis wife, I now realize—steps up to the podium at the front of the ballroom. She smiles gracefully, welcoming everyone and preparing to kick off the charity auction.

But all I can feel is Stephen beside me.

Not touching me.

Not speaking.

Just...there.

He radiates heat, danger, and disappointment. The feeling prickles along my skin like static, making the hair on the back of my neck stand.

My mother sits ramrod straight to my left. My father is on her other side, tracking the room with the alertness of someone who never lowers his guard. He has probably arrested people less suspicious than Stephen.

"Stop looking at him like that," my mother murmurs without turning her head.

"I'm not looking at anyone," I lie. I was looking at Stephen and fighting the urge to reach for him, to touch him.

Damn my inability to not want the bad boy.

Her eyebrow twitches. "You're transparent, dear. It's unbecoming."

I want to roll my eyes. I'm not transparent. I doubt there's anyone in the room who's even noticing me sitting here. I wasn't immune to the lustful glances that Stephen and Lucien both received in this room. There were more brothers— I'd read about them—and no doubt, too, they would turn heads. My mother's concern was unfounded.

Stephen's presence seems to strip away every defense I've relied on my entire life. I'm exposed. Shaken. Too aware of my own needs, warring against what I know is right—what I should do to protect myself and my family.

"So," he finally speaks—quiet, smooth, sliding along my spine like silk and flame. Just a single word, but it has weight. Accusation perhaps? Certainly anger and disappointment are mixed within it. "Are you regretting me?"

My breath catches. I keep my eyes forward, pretending to listen to Briar Moretti discuss bid paddles and donation pledges. "Regretting what?" I don't want to answer. I don't want to admit that a small part of me does regret meeting him. Not because of what we did. No, it's because it'll hurt to walk away. It would be easier on the heart not to start anything. What you don't know can't hurt you, and all that shit.

"You know what." His voice is low enough for my parents to miss, but the tone is intimate. Too intimate. My cheeks burn.

I swallow. Even his voice makes me ache for him. All of him. "I'm not having this conversation here," I whisper back.

"That sounds like a yes."

I grit my teeth. "It's not."

"It feels like it." He leans back in his chair, but his eyes never leave me. "You won't look at me. You pulled away. You introduced me like I'm some guy you bumped into at Starbucks."

"You know why," I snap, keeping my voice low, controlled. "You could've warned me who you were."

"You could've warned me who you were, too." His knee bumps mine under the table—purposeful. "But you didn't."

The worst part? He's right. I've evaded just as much as he has in mentioning my parents, but never telling him who they were or what my father's occupation was. It seemed both of us were wrong on that score.

I suck in a breath, trying to gather the strands of my composure. That I liked Stephen, desired him too, made breaking off whatever we'd started all the harder. "My father hates everything your family represents."

"We don't represent that history any longer. Your father doesn't know me well enough for him to judge." His voice is calm, but the tension simmering under it is sharp enough to cut. "He hates my name. Big difference."

"No," I whisper. "There isn't."

He gives a quiet, humorless laugh. "You think I'm dangerous."

Isn't he? He certainly looks like a man I wouldn't want to cross. "You are dangerous."

"And you like it."

I whip my head toward him. "Stop."

He tilts his head slightly, eyes glinting. "Why? Because it's true?"

My face burns hot enough to light the tablecloth on fire. I check to see if my parents have noticed our hushed conversation, and I'm relieved to see the auction has caught their attention—at least one of the paintings donated has. "This is not the time or place to discuss any of this."

"It's exactly the place."

He shifts closer, barely an inch, but it feels like a gravitational pull I'm helpless against. His hand drifts to my knee under the table, warm and firm and familiar in a way that makes my stomach somersault.

I stiffen immediately. "Don't." My denial of him is more like a breathy plea, hardly a warning.

He starts a slow stroke up the inside of my thigh—a gentle, maddening pass of his thumb. Nothing graphic, nothing overt, but enough to make my lungs seize. I shove his hand off, quick and sharp. My mother glances at me, curious but polite enough not to ask. My father doesn't even turn; he's too busy lifting the auction paddle to try to win a painting for my mother.

Stephen smiles like I've just confirmed some private theory he had about me. "You're blushing," he murmurs.

"Because you're being impossible and trying to embarrass me." *Because I want you, and I'm furious with you at the same time. Why couldn't you be connected to a typical Connecticut family instead of the mafia?* We couldn't be from more opposing back-grounds if we tried.

I don't want boring and normal; I want him. His look, the darkness he exudes, is part of his charm and why I pursued him in the first place. I'm sick of being the good girl and he makes me want to be so very bad.

"I'm being honest."

"You're being reckless and an ass, and you know it."

I meet his gaze. He shrugs. Gah, he's maddening —and why does he have to look so irresistibly sharp in his suit tonight? I want to tear it off him. I want him in my bed. Enough with the car sex—I need all of him.

I close my eyes and fight to control myself. I'm supposed to be breaking it off with this man, not drooling over him.

"You didn't seem to mind reckless the other night. I like it when you take control."

My entire body floods with heat. It's the memory— the grip of his hands on my hips, the soft, shocked sound that escaped my throat when he kissed me, when he thrust deep his very clever cock. The way I let myself unravel in the front seat of his car like a woman who has no responsibilities or consequences.

"Stop," I whisper, desperate. "Please."

He watches me for a long moment. Something cold and wounded flickers across his face. "So you do regret us."

"I..." My throat tightens. "Stephen, my father is the Chief of Police."

"I noticed." His response is dry and dripping with bitterness.

"I'm a lawyer. My whole life, my whole career, everything I've worked for—I can't risk it for—"

"For a Moretti?" he finishes for me, voice flat.

"That's not what I said." I keep thinking, if I could just be certain the Morettis were truly clean—if their family ties to the underworld were really severed— maybe things would be different. But I lost my brother to gang violence. My father serves as a cop. How could I possibly let myself date a man whose life is still entangled in that world?

"It's what you meant."

I shake my head, panicked by how wrong that is— how much I don't want it to be true. "Stephen—"

"No." He leans in, jaw tight. "Say it straight. You think I'll ruin your precious, perfect life. That because I didn't have it as good as you did as a kid, I'm not worthy of you now."

"I don't know what to think." My voice cracks. I hate feeling so confused. "I don't know if you're still involved in your father's world. Or if any of the rumors online are true. Stories link your brother Lucien to Matteo Romero's death. How do I reconcile that when I barely know you?" I pause, reaching for my wine and taking a sip. "Right now, I'm not sure if I like you or if I'm letting lust push me to make stupid decisions."

His hand clamps around mine under the table—not hard, just enough to stop the shaking I didn't realize had started.

"You're not stupid." His voice is steel-wrapped velvet. "Of course, I protect my family, as anyone does, but I won't allow anyone to use me either. Not even you."

"I'm not using you." At least I don't think I have been up until tonight. That isn't who I am, nor who I want to be.

"No? Then what is this?" He nods subtly toward my parents. "You act like you don't know me. Like what happened between us was some accident you want to pretend never happened."

I swallow hard. I knew there had been a possibility that Stephen would be here this evening, but the sight of him had thrown me completely off balance. I would have loved nothing more than to proudly introduce him to my parents, but after my mother met him, her opinion had been set, and my father's soon after. I had hoped he'd ignore my presence, saving me from having to distance myself in front of my family, if only to save them the worry, but in turn, and by doing so, I'd hurt Stephen.

"I don't want to pretend. I just—Stephen, I'm trying to protect myself and my family just as you do."

"From me."

"From everything," I whisper. "From what this could do to my family, to my job, to my reputation—"

"And what about what it does to you?" he asks quietly. "You think I haven't noticed the way you look at me?"

"Stephen—" It's pointless arguing. I *do* look at him. I want him every second of every hour, and that no doubt was conveyed on my face. Hell, even my mother noticed this evening...

"The way you fall apart when I kiss you. That has to be worth fighting for."

I feel like the air has been vacuumed out of the room. Beside me, my mother lifts her wineglass, oblivious. "You're being cruel," I whisper.

"No," he says. "I'm being fair. I'm asking you to own it. Own what you want."

Tears sting the backs of my eyes. Not because he's wrong. But because he's too close to being right. I pull my hand out of his slowly and sit up straighter. "This isn't a fair conversation."

"Life isn't fair."

"Not like this." My voice shakes. "Not with my parents right here. Not with everything at stake. You can't corner me like this." I wanted out of the conversation and, at this point, I'd say anything for it to end—for us to just sit quietly and ignore everything that sits between us.

He watches me, eyes dark and unreadable. "Then tell me not to try."

I stare at him. I can't say that. I *need* to—I know I do—but to form those words...impossible.

Something shifts between us. Something heavy and inevitable. Briar's voice rings out over the speakers as another auction item appears on the screen, but I hear none of it. Not a word. I'm too busy drowning in the look Stephen gives me—hungry, angry, wounded, determined.

I can't sit here another second.

"I need air," I murmur abruptly, pushing my chair back and fleeing as if the hounds of hell are on my heels.

My mother glances over, surprised. "Are you all right, darling? You look flushed."

"I'm fine," I lie. "I'll be back momentarily."

Stephen rises with me instantly, ignoring my silent plea for him to stay seated.

"Where are you going?" my father asks, suspicion slicing into his voice.

"Restroom," I say, not wanting my father to follow me—not if Stephen seems determined to also.

Stephen adds, "I'll show you where they are."

My father's jaw clenches, but he can't object without causing a scene—and my family never causes scenes.

I turn sharply, not trusting myself to breathe if I stay another second. "Fine," I hiss.

Stephen follows, his steps unhurried, confident. Infuriating.

When we're far enough from the dining room, I grab his hand—not because I want to, but because if I don't drag him, he'll take his merry time on purpose. His palm is warm, solid, too familiar.

We step out of the room and into a long, softly lit hallway, lined with framed posters of past charity events. The door closes behind us with a soft thud.

Silence.

Heavy.

Loaded.

I drop his hand immediately and whirl toward him. "What was that? Back there?"

He watches me with a slow, predatory calm that makes my pulse trip. Damn him for making me want him without even trying. I don't know what pull he has over me, but this can't end well.

"Me trying to figure out if you're running from yourself or from me."

"That's not fair, and you know it. We hardly suit; our families couldn't be more opposite. If we end it now, no one gets hurt."

"So we're pleasing everyone else but ourselves," he counters, voice low. "Sounds pretty shit to me."

"No, it's for the best." I know I'm trying to convince myself, but all I want is him. The war within me is nothing I've ever known, nor do I know how to navigate my conflicted thoughts.

"Maybe it is." He steps closer. "Or maybe I'm just not letting our families decide what happens between us."

"Stephen—"

He stops right in front of me. Too close. Too much. "I'm not walking away from you," he says quietly. "Even if you think you should walk away from me."

I inhale sharply, my chest tight with panic and longing. I don't know how to separate. "Stephen..." My voice trembles. "Don't do this."

He sinks slowly—deliberately—down onto his knees.

Right here.

In front of me.

In the quiet, empty hall.

My breath shatters, and the world tilts. "Get up," I order.

He shakes his head. "No."

THIRTEEN

STEPHEN

I DON'T GIVE A FUCK WHO MAY CATCH US, ALL I care about at this moment is making Dallen remember who we are and what we're starting to mean to each other. There is something special—I can *feel* it whenever I'm around her—and nothing, not her high-and-mighty mother or her law-abiding father will change that.

I lift her gown. She's so utterly beautiful this evening that my chest hurts. I kiss along her leg, feeling her tremble under my touch. Her fingers glide into my hair. I expect her to push me away, but she doesn't. Instead, she holds me against her. The distant hum of the ballroom filters down the hallway, muffled applause and clinking glasses echoing faintly. She leans back against the wall, and I know she's mine.

Mine to fucking eat.

I reach under her gown and pull her panties down. They settle at her ankles, and she lifts one foot to free herself from them. "Put your leg on my shoulder, Pumpkin."

She doesn't argue. Instead she watches me while she does as I tell her.

Good girl...

"Stephen, not here. We'll be caught, and the scandal will be ridiculous." There's amusement in her voice, and very little denial in her body.

I smile against the skin on her leg, kissing my way along her thigh. Her skin is so soft, and damn, she smells so good. Warm lighting from the sconces casts a low, golden glow over her skin, making her look ethereal. "I don't care who catches us. I have to taste you, remind you that you belong to me now."

I feel her still at my words, but I don't stop kissing toward her sex. Almost there. My mouth waters at the thought of licking her pretty cunt.

"I don't belong to you or anyone."

I ignore her words, let her believe what she wants, but she is mine. She's been mine since the moment I took her virginity. Hell, the moment I saw her in the nightclub. And I had seen her first, even if she never knew that fact.

I push her dress up to her hips and pin her against

the wall with my hands. She sucks in a startled breath as my tongue glides along her opening.

I groan. Just as I thought—sweet as sin on the palate.

My cock presses hard against my pants. I'm going to take her back to my place tonight, and I'm going to fuck her in my bed, lay claim to her once and for all.

But now—right at this moment—it's her turn to enjoy. To revel in what I can do for her. I slip two fingers into her tight cunt, tease her as I suckle her clit. She undulates against my mouth, seeking release, and I'm going to give it to her.

"Stephen..." Her breathy moan makes my head spin. Damn, I like the sound of my name on her lips. It's like the purest cocaine in the world, the best high a person can have.

I lick her good, suckle that sweet button relentlessly until she shatters in my arms. I hold her upright, allow the tremors to subside, her pleasure to wane, before I, with one last kiss on her thigh, pull back and help put her panties back into place.

The sight of her, allowing me the privilege of touching her so intimately, shatters something cold and dark within me, and I know I can't allow anything to come between us.

I've fucked a lot of women, but Dallen... Dallen is my endgame.

I stand and adjust her gown, brushing a stray curl from her cheek. Her breathing softens, the flush in her skin slowly fading. Down the hall, the ballroom noise grows louder—auctioneer chatter, claps, laughter— reminding us we're expected back.

"Ready?" I murmur.

She nods, still a little shaky. I take her hand, guiding her gently as we walk back toward the double doors. The moment we step inside, bright lights and the swell of voices swallow us.

And that's when Alex Romero appears.

He materializes suddenly before us, blocking our path, a glass of champagne in hand, smiling widely like we're old friends. We're far from friends and I don't want him or his kind anywhere near me or Dallen.

I stiffen, fight not to rip the bastard's smug head off when he leans in and kisses Dallen's cheek, bold enough to make my blood boil.

Careful, Romero...

"Dallen," he drawls. "You look stunning this evening. Glad to see you here tonight. I did wonder if you and your family would be on the guest list."

I force myself to stay polite but can't hide my disdain. I crack my neck, the tension coiling within me wanting an outlet. Preferably, a fist to Romero's nose.

"Mr. Romero," Dallen says, surprise in her voice. "Good evening to you."

I clear my throat, wrapping my arm around Dallen's waist and pulling her close. "And you know each other how?" I ask, unsure how Dallen could have crossed paths with this family, and yet, here we were.

"Redwood and Tully are our new law firm, Dallen is our contact there," Alex says, too friendly, too bold for my liking. "Elio and my family feel most fortunate to have such an accomplished and well-respected lawyer and firm behind us."

Their lawyer.

Alex reaches out and brushes a hand along Dallen's arm like he has any fucking right.

I ground my teeth and stare at Romero until he gets the hint to back the fuck off. He catches my eye and whatever he sees in mine is enough that he heeds my silent threat. Alex smiles, tight and sharp.

"We need to get back to our table," I say, moving Dallen before she's had a chance to wish our unwanted guest a good evening.

I guide her back to our seats—right beside her parents—ignoring their displeasure that Dallen and I are at least back on speaking terms. Little do they know we're on a lot more terms than that.

I cross the room to where Alex and Elio sit, their false laughter and enjoyment for the evening like nails scoring down a chalkboard. When I reach their table, I pull out the empty chair beside Alex and sit down without permission.

Not that I need any.

"Evening, gentlemen."

Elio straightens a little too fast, betraying nerves. Alex tries for a charming grin, but it twitches unsteadily at the edges. "Stephen. To what do we owe the pleasure?"

"You seem too familiar with your lawyer," I say. "Let's clear that up."

Alex shrugs. "Just a friendly greeting, nothing more. We're building rapport."

My smile widens yet I feel no mirth. I feel like slamming the bastard's head into the table and stabbing him with the dessert spoon. "Professional relationships don't involve you putting your mouth on her."

Alex swallows and I can almost hear his nerves. Jaw flexing, he glances away momentarily.

Good. I want him to feel uncomfortable. I want him to know he doesn't touch what is mine or he'll end up as dead as his cousin.

Elio cuts in, tone smoother, as if he's going to console my fury with his words.

Idiot.

"Stephen, lad...we meant no disrespect. Miss Byrne is...impressive. Skilled. Sharp. And honestly?

Surprisingly brave, not to mention extremely pleasant to be around."

My jaw ticks. I know pleasant means she's nice on the eye, and Dallen is, but she's nice on my eyes, no one else's. "Brave?" I mention. "How so?"

Alex leans back, lacing his fingers over his stomach. "Well, you know. Considering who she's dating." His eyes glitter and my fingers twitch to strike. "Walking into the lion's den without even knowing she's a juicy piece of meat."

A cold, controlled fury threads through me. "Careful, Romero."

"We're being friendly, that's all," Alex says, voice too casual and high to be honest. He looks to Elio as if he's said nothing wrong. Oh, he's said something wrong and he'll pay for it, one way or another. I'll make sure of that.

"Friendly," I repeat, pretending to digest the word. "Is that what we're calling it?"

Elio leans forward as if we're enjoying our combined conversation. We are not. "You bring a woman into your life—she falls right into our world. Call it fate that's she's also useful...for now."

Oh, hell no.

Some would call that a threat.

I call it a threat.

"And some," I say, voice glacial, "would call that

suicide, because that's what it would be to say such things to a Moretti."

Alex tilts his head. "Depends on who you ask. We're businessmen. We look for opportunities as do you and your brothers."

Opportunities?

I know exactly what that means. "You think touching her is leverage? That by hiring her firm it enables you to get close to her to do her harm." I shake my head, my blood pumping loud in my ears.

I cannot kill them here. We're at a charity auction. It would ruin the family if society watched me dispose of these two goons before them all.

"No, boys, that path merely ends with you buried in an unknown, unmarked grave. Don't try it."

Elio's mouth twitches. "We'll take your words under consideration."

My blood turns to ice, a cold weight settles in my veins as realization dawns that they don't care. That they either think I'm bluffing, or we're not cut from the same cloth as our father. How wrong they are. I lean in, close enough they can feel the warning radiate off me. "You go near her again. You breathe in her vicinity. You speak her name and I'll crack this city open, bury you and your entire bloodline beneath the rubble, name carved in stone as a warning to anyone else who thinks to test me."

Alex blinks slowly. "Touchy."

Elio murmurs, "She must be something—got that Moretti fire burning. Matteo would love to see it, but alas," he says with a sigh. "He can't, can he, because he's dead."

I force my expression to stay calm even as my pulse roars. "This isn't about Matteo, he has nothing to do with anything, not us and no longer you."

"Oh, we disagree," Alex says quietly. "You killed him. Or your brother did. Or both, doesn't matter to be honest, but my point is—we haven't forgotten, and we don't forgive."

I smile coldly. "Don't start something that won't end well for you."

Their eyes flare with hate.

Good. They need the warning. Idiots think I'm bluffing. They have no idea what me and my family are capable of when one of our own is threatened. And Dallen, she's mine, not theirs to toy with, injure or kill.

Mine...

"Last warning, boys. Stay away from Dallen. Don't poke a bear you can't outrun."

Alex grins. "We'll stay away if she does. She's our lawyer—hard to avoid." He shrugs. "Want her to drop us? That'd be a disappointment to her bosses and may be hard to accomplish."

My muscles lock, tension racing through me as my

eyes narrow. And for the first time, they know it. They know I can't control everything, certainly not her bosses nor her family, who are hell bent on ridding me from her life.

Elio raises his glass. "To our new legal counsel. And to you, Stephen. Congratulations. It seems you've got yourself a woman worth bleeding for."

Alex adds, "And a woman worth taking, if someone wanted revenge."

I stand so suddenly that both men flinch. "That will never happen."

Alex smiles slowly. "Then you better make damn sure she's kept safe. Lots of dangers in New York. Murder capital of the world the last I heard. So many missing women, quite sad really," he says, nonchalant.

I walk away before I pick up the spoon and scoop their eyes from their heads. My jaw clenches so tight it aches, every instinct sharpened to a blade. They think they found a way to drag us back into war. Over my dead, shattered body.

Or over theirs first.

FOURTEEN

DALLEN

Stephen returns to the table with the kind of barely leashed energy that sets my nerves on edge. The auction is winding down, the low buzz of conversation rising again as everyone shifts in their seats, ready for the dance to begin afterward. I reach for my glass of wine, needing to calm my nerves after what we just did before dessert is served. My mother is chatting with the couple beside her, my father is speaking with a local councilman, and, for a rare moment, no one is paying attention to what's happening between Stephen and me.

Except the man himself, of course. He's so intense, so engaged that it's a little intimidating and not what I'm used to.

He sits beside me without a word. His arm brushes mine, and even that small contact feels electrified. My pulse jumps, stupidly hopeful at the idea that the storm between us might finally be passing.

But when he turns to me, the tension in his jaw tells me otherwise.

"You're not working with them." His words are low, urgent.

I blink. "Excuse me?"

"The Romeros, you can't work for them. I forbid it."

My stomach contracts painfully. He forbids it. I almost scoff at his gumption to say such a thing to a woman he's known for all of five minutes. Seriously, the man needs to read the room. "I don't think what I do at my work is relevant, nor is it appropriate or allowed for me to discuss my clients. What I do at Redwood and Tully is none of your business, and neither is their choice on who we pick up and represent."

His nostrils flare, and I ignore the nerves that settle in my stomach. I know, somehow deep within me, that he wouldn't hurt me, punish me for being disobedient, but still, he's an intimidating man, and it takes a lot to stand up for what I know is right, not just for my employment, but for me. I cannot allow him to think he can rule me.

"No," I cut in, voice tight. "My job isn't up for

debate, Stephen. We've known each other for five minutes. My clients have nothing to do with this."

His eyes narrow—like he's trying to choose his words carefully while keeping his composure. "They're not good men, Dallen."

I can figure that out myself and don't need anyone to tell me. After I'm given a case, I research the family. Law firms don't just represent clean parties. Some of the wealthiest people in the world are far from clean; the Romeros are no different.

"Well, I'm not in the business of judging clients, that's for a jury or judge to do. And I'm merely looking into their assets, so their character has no bearing on me." I keep my voice low and controlled, but irritation crawls up my spine. "And unless you have a conviction or a legal document to drop in front of me, I can't exactly go to my boss and tell him I won't touch a new account because someone I'm dating thinks they're shady."

"It's not jealousy," he says, calm steel in his voice. "It's knowing they're dangerous."

I stare at him. "You're being dramatic."

"Am I?" His fingers curl slightly against his thigh. "You have no idea what kind of people they are."

"And you conveniently won't tell me," I snap back. "Do you see the problem there? You want me to drop clients based on vibes and jealousy."

His eyes flash. "This isn't jealousy."

"Oh, it absolutely is," I hiss. "The moment Alex kissed my cheek, you looked like you wanted to flip a table."

"He shouldn't have touched you."

"And you don't get to decide that," I fire back. "You don't get to control my job, my clients, or who greets me politely at a charity gala." Even though my skin crawled when Alex kissed me, leaving me feeling suddenly dirty and in need of a shower. I shudder at the thought and reach for my wine again.

He leans close, his breath brushing my neck, and now I shiver for another reason altogether. "They weren't being polite."

I grit my teeth, trying to ignore the fact this man fires up my soul like no one else. "Until something's legally problematic, until my managing partner says otherwise, I'm not dropping them. End of conversation."

He stares at me, fury simmering beneath the surface. But there's something else too—fear? No, not fear. Concern. Something heavier. I don't let myself soften. Not tonight. If I do, I'll be controlled by him for the foreseeable future, or however long this—whatever we have—lasts, and I can't allow that.

The final auction paddle drops. Applause ripples through the room. My mother stands to clap, and my father laughs at something the gentleman beside him says. Stephen turns toward me, and for a moment, everything in the world quiets.

"I want you to come home with me tonight," he murmurs.

My breath hitches. "Stephen—"

"I'm not asking for forever. Just...don't leave tonight like this. We need to talk, and I want you in my bed. I'm not hiding that fact."

God help me, I should say no. I should walk out and put every wall back up. But the ache between us tightens my chest, the unresolved heat makes my skin flush, and the still-burning argument creates a restless energy inside me. All of it pulls me toward him, against every rational thought.

And I say the word I shouldn't.

"Fine."

His shoulders ease minutely, but his eyes remain dark, unreadable. He reaches for my hand beneath the table, and even though I should pull away, I don't.

We leave separately after he texts me his address. Optics, of course. My parents would probably have a stroke if they saw us leave together. He waits for me outside his apartment, and I see him kicking his heels as my taxi pulls up. We don't speak as he takes my hand and we enter the building and ride the elevator up. The energy between us is too volatile, too loaded.

My stomach is in knots, anticipation tightening every muscle. My blood pounds in my ears, and I can still feel the echo of his touch from earlier. Desire thrums through me, sharper for having him here, finally alone in the quiet of his home—free from interruption, free to give in to whatever we want.

Damn, I have it bad...

By the time we reach his apartment, my pulse has become a frantic, nervous flutter. The space is warm, dimly lit, and expensive without being sterile. He pours wine without asking, hands me a glass, watches me take off my heels and curl my toes against one of his rugs.

Maybe it's the wine, maybe I'm exhausted, or maybe I'm just done fighting for tonight. Frustration and weariness settle over me as I tuck myself into the corner of his couch, letting my head fall back against the cushion, wishing for a moment of peace.

He sits at the opposite end, angled toward me, glass in hand, eyes still burning with everything left unsaid.

For a few minutes, neither of us speaks. Then he breaks the peaceful silence, and I inwardly groan at the loss of calm.

"You shouldn't work with them, Dallen."

And just like that, my spine stiffens. "We're not doing this again. I can't do what you want, Stephen. End of conversation."

"We are discussing this further." His voice is softer than before, but more dangerous too. His quiet calm is more terrifying than his loud, abrupt manner. "I'm not going to pretend this is fine."

"Well, it's not your call."

"It is when it involves you."

"No," I say firmly, shaking my head. I sit up and place my wine on the coffee table. "No, Stephen. You don't get to decide which clients my firm takes on or which cases I work on. You don't get to insert yourself into my job because you don't like someone."

His jaw flexes. "It's not about like."

"Then give me information," I challenge. "Real information. Something other than 'trust me, they're bad.' I can't act on gut feelings. You're asking me to compromise my professional ethics based on what—a look? A warning you won't explain?" His silence is infuriating. "Exactly," I say. "You don't get to ask that of me. Not now. Not ever." I stand and start putting on my shoes. "I'm going home."

He stands instantly. "Dallen."

"No. I'm not going to sit here and let you dictate my life." When I turn to leave, his hand closes around my wrist, firm enough to stop me. He pulls me against his chest, and I lose my balance and tumble into him. Straight into his lap.

I gasp as one arm sits against my waist, while the

other slides across my thigh, fingers tracing slow, consuming lines that melt through my anger like heat through ice.

"Don't walk away from me." His voice is low, rough silk against my back. "Not when you don't mean it."

"I do mean it," I murmur, despite my body's response—my pulse races and my skin prickles under his touch. Pulled by conflicting feelings, I crave him even as I try to muster resistance. Deep down, I know he's blurring boundaries, using my desire to win me over—but I tell myself I'm stronger than this, even while my resolve shakes with longing.

I am.

"You're angry," he says quietly. "I get it. But I'm not trying to control your job. I'm trying to keep you safe."

"That's not your responsibility. I have enough of that with my father. I don't need it from the man I'm fucking as well."

He growls, and I'm not sure if he's pissed or it's because I rolled my hips against his engorged cock. "It became my responsibility the second you walked into my life."

His hand sweeps higher, brushing my breast, and my breath hitches, my resolve trembles. "Stephen," I whisper, "this isn't how you win an argument."

"I'm not trying to win." His lips brush my shoulder. "I'm trying to keep you."

A shiver runs through me—want and fury tangled so tightly I can't separate them. I shouldn't be with this man. Guilt stabs at me, and fear simmers beneath my longing. Everything that makes us who we are, our past, our future, nothing meshes, and yet, I can't seem to pull away. "You can't keep me from doing my job," I manage, my voice trembling.

"I know," he murmurs. "But I can show you how much you matter to me."

And God help me...I let him. I let myself lean against his chest, his hands coaxing, distracting, soothing, and infuriating all at once. I let myself breathe him in, let the heat of him blur the sharp edges of my irritation. I let myself forget, for one dangerous moment, that the world outside his apartment that's waiting to tear us apart doesn't exist.

But it does.

FIFTEEN

STEPHEN

I'm going to keep her forever and be damned what anyone else thinks of the matter. I'll raise hell with anyone who gets in my way. The city hums faintly beyond the apartment walls, distant sirens and traffic muffled by glass and height.

Dallen is mine, and she, too, will soon come to realize that we're made for each other. We click. The chemistry between us is off the charts. Nothing can change that, not even how much she loves her family.

In the end, she'll choose me. I have to believe that, or I'll go insane. Because the alternative—her walking away, choosing her father's world over mine—is something I don't know how to survive.

I play her body like an instrument, tease her breasts, roll my fingers around her nipples, and relish her sexy little squirm on my lap that presses against my cock. I'm going to fuck her so hard, control her like a toy. God help me, she feels like something I can lose, and that thought claws at my chest.

"Stephen..." Her breathy moan fires my blood more. I pick her up around her waist and set her on her hands and knees on the lounge. I kneel behind her, the need burning through me like a wildfire I'm unable to control.

I push up her dress, her pretty, tight ass in her sexy thong greeting me. I lean down and kiss one cheek, sliding her silk panties off to pool at her knees. She shivers, and I can see she's wet. I dip a finger into her cunt, twist it to tease her G-spot. She moans, gasps at my intrusion into her body, but squirms with need. Acceptance.

My cock hardens further. I rip my pants open, my large dick pressing Dallen's sex as if it knows where paradise lies. I push into her, watching as I stretch her slick warmth, taking me fully. I remain still a moment, enjoying her heat as it tightens around me, contracts, seeking release.

Damn, she feels good.

I pull out and thrust hard, claiming her body. I clasp her hips, moan as she cries out my name, muffled into the lounge. "That's it, Pumpkin. Enjoy me."

"Yes..." Her cries spur me on, and I lunge into her again.

She's so wet, ready, needy. I love it. Every moment of it. My balls ache, my stomach is a knot of need, of wants and desires. She makes me feel so much more than anyone before. Too much. Enough that I can see how badly this can destroy me if she decides I'm not worth the risk.

I cannot get enough of her.

"Tell me you're mine. That you'll not allow anything to come between us."

She moans, a sound that's tinged with want and frustration. "I can't," she says, still denying me what I want. Still refusing to believe what I say is true. Still holding herself apart from me, as if she might bolt at any moment.

I punish her by pulling out. I sit, hard as rock against her ass, and reach around and roll my fingers against her clit. She moans, squirms against my hand. "Tell me, Dallen. Say you'll keep seeing me, no matter what anyone else says. We're good together." I slip my fingers between her slick folds, dipping them into her moist heat before rolling them over her button.

"Stephen, stop teasing. I can't take it."

She presses her ass against my cock, and I undulate against her. I want to come. I want her to agree to what I'm ordering her to do. She's so frustratingly independent, a trait I'm finding a fucking turn-on and dangerous, because independence means she can choose to walk away—from me, from my name, from everything I am.

"Tell me you'll drop the Romeros as clients."

She moans, and I thrust into her once more, taking her, owning her. She pushes back against me, sitting up and facing forward on my lap. I clasp one of her tits, teasing her pebbled nipple as I grind my fingers around her clit. She tightens about my cock, the tremors of her forthcoming release dragging me into joining her.

The Romeros shouldn't be anywhere near her. They don't touch what's mine. They don't circle something I care about without consequences.

"You like me fucking owning you. Admit it."

"I love this," she stubbornly says. "But you'll never own me, Stephen."

I pinch her clit before rolling it under the pads of my fingers. She lets out a squeal of pain mixed with pleasure before she comes. Her body convulses around my cock, and I'm powerless to stop my release.

I thrust into her, wanting my seed deep, to claim. Not that I think anything will come of it. She's a sensible woman. She is more than protected, even if I'm not.

"Stephen," she screams, her head pressing against my shoulder. I kiss her neck, relishing the feel of our orgasm ripping through us both. Her father will hate this. The Romeros will use it. And still, I can't make myself stop.

"Dallen," I groan. The urge to never let her go, to keep her here with me, safe and not around those who will keep us apart, is overwhelming. But there isn't a war I haven't yet won, and I always get what I want. The Moretti's don't lose.

And I won't lose Dallen.

SIXTEEN

DALLEN

By Monday morning, I'm convincing myself that the charity auction is a fever dream and my night in Stephen's arms afterward as well—too much socializing, too much champagne, too much Stephen. If I focus hard enough on my work, maybe I can shrink the memory of his hands on my body, the way he kneels in front of me in the hallway, the way I almost—almost—let myself forget who he is when I go back to his apartment.

Almost cave and give in to what he wants me to do.

Be owned by him?

Part of me wants to be kept, to be owned by him, but not in the way he wants. I want love, companionship, trust, and loyalty. I don't want to be told what I can and can't do, and I'll never settle for scraps. I deserve so much more than that, and I don't care how much bad blood runs between him and the Romeros, that has nothing to do with me.

A knock sounds on my door, and I look up expecting to see my assistant. Instead, it's my father. He steps through the doorway of my office, fills the frame like a storm cloud—broad-shouldered, imposing, wearing the expression he saves for briefing homicide detectives. My stomach drops.

"Dad?" I stand too quickly. "Is everything okay?"

"We need to talk," he says.

That tone. My pulse stutters. I sit down, trying not to imagine the worst. "Is Mom okay?" I ask.

"She's fine, this call isn't about her." He doesn't sit, he plants his hands on the back of the chair opposite my desk, head lowered, gathering himself. This is bad. I brace myself for whatever it is he's about to say.

"Dallen," he says finally, lifting his gaze. "I've been made aware of something."

The dread pools in my gut. "What?"

"Your clients. The Romeros."

I blink—dear Lord, not him as well. I fight not to sigh, to tell him to leave, but something stops me. He is the Chief of Police. Maybe he knows something with truth behind its claims. "What about them?" I say, knowing I must tread carefully regarding client confidentiality.

His jaw flexes. "Do you know what they want with

you? The true reason why they hired Redwood & Tully?"

"What do they want with me?" I repeat, shaking my head, "Dad, I'm their attorney. What else would they want than representation?"

He straightens, all business now. "We intercepted a conversation this morning. Wiretap on one of their associates. They're not hiring your firm because they care about Matteo's assets." He pauses. "They're using the firm to get close to you because you're getting close to someone they want to hurt."

A chill darts down my spine. "Why would—?"

He cuts me off. "They know you're seeing Stephen Moretti, and if they weren't sure before, they certainly are now after the charity event Saturday night."

My legs shake, and I grip the edge of my desk. "That's—no. Dad, I barely know Stephen Moretti. We haven't even discussed if we're exclusive." Although, after what Stephen said to me the other night, I'm pretty sure he's already under the assumption we're a couple and I'm exclusive. His possessive nature toward me already should raise red flags, yet I know he wouldn't hurt me. That doesn't mean he wouldn't hurt others who threaten our relationship.

Are the Romeros up to no good? Am I a pawn in their game? Is Stephen correct?

My father's fingers tighten on the back of the chair,

his knuckles turning white. "It doesn't matter what you've discussed. They think you're connected to him, and intimately, all the better for them." He shakes his head, looking weary and concerned. "These mobsters have one rule they enjoy enforcing most. An eye for an eye. They believe the Morettis killed one of their own, and you, being with Stephen..." His nostrils flare. "You're a target of opportunity."

My heart pounds so hard I feel it in my fingertips. "Dad, this doesn't make sense. Why would they come after me over something that isn't even proven, and isn't even being investigated? If law enforcement thought the Morettis had killed a Romero, I would think that would be headline news."

"Nothing the mafia does needs to make sense," he snaps. "It doesn't have to be logical. It just has to hurt."

What my father says slowly sinks in. "Oh my God."

His expression softens, taking on a tinge of fear. I've only seen my father look like that once: when my brother was killed.

"This is not a game, Dallen." His voice breaks through my spiraling thoughts. "These people don't care about your career, your future, your safety, or any of us. They see you as leverage. As punishment."

A thick knot forms in my throat. "What do I do? I can't just drop them as clients. My boss is so pleased to have picked them up. There will be questions that I'm not sure they'll believe should I tell them, especially when some of the information is a father's fear."

"In either case, you're going to talk to whomever you need to," he says firmly. "To drop them as clients. Immediately."

I nod, because what else can I do? "All right. Instead of the information you've come into, I'll tell them today and inform the Romeros before the close of office."

He exhales, the sound one of relief. "Good." Another pause, and then—softer, but somehow heavier — "There's something else."

Of course there is.

I brace myself.

"I want you to stop seeing him."

The words hit like a slap. "Dad—"

"I'm not negotiating on this."

Anger flashes through me, sharp and defensive. "You can't tell me who I can date." It's bad enough that he's telling me who my clients can be, even though intelligence has alerted them that the Romeros are up to no good. Still, it irks. As a Taurus, I loathe being told what I can and can't do.

"I can tell you who's dangerous." His jaw tightens. "Stephen's father is a renowned killer. Ruthless. Sadistic. I put men in the ground because of him. And the

Moretti wealth—" He gestures broadly. "It isn't built on shipping, construction, and real estate. It's built on blood."

I shake my head. "That was decades ago. Everything I've read says the brothers are legitimate, everything's above board." I pause, softening my tone. "Dad, you can't keep punishing children for the sins of their father. That's not fair."

"That's what they want the world to think," he says coldly. "But these men don't change, Dallen. Violence is their language. Their inheritance. They are cut from the same cloth. Don't be fooled, they're not."

I look away, throat tightening. I want to argue. God, I want to scream that Stephen isn't like that. That he's intense, yes—volatile, yes—but he's also gentle with me. Real. Honest in a way that others haven't been. Still, there's a grain of truth to what my father says. I saw it Saturday night when Stephen was near the Romeros. An old hate, as cold as ice that will never be thawed. Not by either family.

"Dad, I hear you," I say quietly. "I do. But I don't know what you expect me to do."

He pulls out the chair and sits. "I expect you to end it. Now. Today. Let him know it's over, and then you walk away." His eyes harden. "I'm not losing you to the same brutal world that killed Daniel. I won't."

I close my eyes, overwhelmed. I don't respond—not yes, not no—and that seems to be enough for him.

He lets out a slow breath and reaches for my hand. "Drop the Romeros as clients. Cut ties with the Moretti boy. And stay alert. I mean it."

I nod mutely.

He leaves then, satisfied he's delivered some paternal decree that will fix everything, as if the world bends to his willpower.

When the door closes, the silence is suffocating.

I lean back into my chair fully, pressing my palms to my face. My thoughts are a snarled mess—fear, desire, resentment, confusion, the memory of Stephen burning through the haze.

I should end it. I know that. Just days ago, I was going to. But then the charity event happened. Stephen happened, and I let myself want—really want—something reckless and wild and utterly wrong.

He's dangerous.

He's intoxicating.

He's everything I shouldn't touch.

But when he's with me, when he kisses me, when he looks at me like I'm the only person he's ever wanted—I feel alive in a way I never have. And that scares me more than the Romeros.

I stare blankly at the case files scattered across my desk, unable to focus on a single word.

I don't know what to do. I don't know what I *should* do. My phone buzzes.

I swear my heart stops when I see his name.

> Looking forward to seeing you tonight.

I grip the phone so tightly my knuckles ache. And I realize—I'm nowhere near ready to let him go, no matter the danger that could lurk by dating a Moretti.

SEVENTEEN

STEPHEN

Alex, the damn Romero raises his glass in my direction from the bar. The smug bastard, like this is all just a game to him. We'll see how much he likes to play when I knock his turkey teeth down his thick throat.

That look — the deliberate confidence, the way he angles his body, cocky and self-assured as if he's untouchable. I know what he's doing. He's taunting me that he's working with Dallen while knowing she's mine.

And I don't share.

I take a deep breath and glance at the woman at his side. I haven't seen her before, but that doesn't mean anything. Is she Alex's girl? If so, maybe a threat toward her will keep the Romeros in line if they decide to step over the one I've drawn.

I glance at Lucien and Anthony, who are more

than aware of who's in this bar with us. My attention snags on Anthony.

He goes rigid like he's seen a ghost.

Anthony doesn't get rattled. He doesn't freeze. He doesn't lose control. He's been in rooms with men who would skin him alive without blinking and walked out calm as a priest after confession.

But this?

This has knocked the breath out of him, and that scares me far more than Alex Romero ever could.

"Didn't think Alex Romero could pull any woman. Seems I'm wrong?" Lucien mutters.

I don't answer because I'm too busy watching Anthony's face as recognition flickers there — sharp, unmistakable — followed by something else entirely.

Regret.

Shit.

Alex's voice carries easily over the many people occupying the bar. "Gentlemen. Didn't expect to see you here." Of course you did, you lying fuck. He steps nearer, as if we want to have a conversation with him. We don't.

"This is my sister," he adds smoothly. "Isabella." He pauses. "Thought you'd be out with Miss Byrne this evening, Stephen. You should keep an eye on that one. She's special."

Special?

The word lands wrong. Too rehearsed. Too convenient. "Your sister," I say, returning fire, letting the dick know such information is also useful." Not that I knew the goon has a sister, Matteo certainly never showcased the female cousin. Not once. Not in years of underworld dealings, surveillance, whispers. In our types of families, you don't just forget to mention a sibling or cousin unless you've kept them hidden for a reason.

That she's being showcased is...odd.

Anthony pushes back from the table so abruptly that his chair flips onto the floor. "I need air," he mutters, already turning away.

I watch him go, unease crawling up my spine. That reaction isn't just surprise, that's history.

Lucien leans in. "You clock that?"

"Yes," I say quietly. "And I don't like it." Not one fucking bit. Is there a history here between Anthony and this Isabella we aren't aware of? We may not know now, but we damn well will soon enough.

Alex catches my eye and smiles wider, like he knows he's just thrown two grenades into the middle of our table. He knows exactly what he's done, and my ire doubles. I'm going to enjoy making the motherfucker into pulp.

"He's taunting me," I murmur. "Letting me know they're watching, aware of our movements and Dallen's. I don't like it."

Lucien nods slowly. "They're certainly sending a message."

My grip tightens around my glass. "They know Dallen matters to me." And that's a problem. I've spent my entire adult life making sure no one can ever use something I love against me. Properties can burn. Deals can collapse. Even family understands the cost of the life we were born into.

But Dallen?

She didn't choose this. She didn't grow up learning how to read danger in a man's eyes or measure exits the second she walks into a room. She trusts contracts. Rules. Systems. The law, first and foremost. And those things don't mean a damn thing to men like the Romeros.

To men like me...

"He thinks she makes me vulnerable," I say. And perhaps in a small way, she does. To care for someone means to be exposed, something I've never allowed myself before. But maybe it's more than that—more than I even want to admit myself.

Lucien studies me. "Does she?"

I don't answer right away, because the profound truth scares the hell out of me. Yes, she does. She makes me hesitate. Makes me think before acting. Makes me imagine consequences beyond survival, dominance, and winning. She makes me want something clean in a world that's never been clean.

She makes me want to be a better man. The type of man I've been fighting to become ever since our father died.

"She makes me careful," I say finally, not wanting to admit to everything coiling about me inside.

Lucien exhales. "Then she's in danger."

I fist my hands, fighting not to remove that danger, the one in front of me now, no matter who was around. "I know..."

Anthony returns, face tight, eyes darker than before. "Another round, boys," he says flatly. We look at him, and he knows we want to ask about this Isabella he's reacted so badly to, but now isn't the time.

"Sure, sounds good," I agree.

My mind races, connections forming whether I want them to or not. The Romeros are hiring Dallen. Alex is being bold with her at the gala. Showing up here with a sister no one knew existed.

They're circling and playing games.

I think of Dallen at the charity event, sitting stiff beside her parents, trying to pretend her life isn't suddenly intersecting with mine in ways she can't fully understand. Think of the way she bristles when I question her work, how fiercely she guards her independence, how she'll hate that I need her to listen to me, to reason, and drop the Romeros as clients.

Stay with me no matter the risk.

"How do I make her see sense?" I say to both Lucien and Anthony, the words rougher than I intend. "Without scaring her off?" If I haven't scared her off already. I was forceful the last time we were together, trying to control her, make her do what I want through sex.

I grind my teeth, hating that I reverted to such underhanded coercion while knowing full well that I'd do it again in a heartbeat.

Lucien's gaze softens just a fraction. "You stop lying and tell her everything. Every dirty, dark secret our family has, and why she must know to keep her safe."

That lands hard.

"You tell her enough truth that she can then protect herself and choose what she wants to do," he continues. "And you accept the risk that she might walk."

The idea makes my chest constrict, because I already know how that will go. Dallen will choose her world, the law over lawlessness. If she walks away from me, it won't be because she doesn't want me, but because she's afraid of what loving me could cost.

Not an outcome I'll allow. I can't let her go. I won't.

"She's a keeper, and if after seeing you at the charity event is any indication, you want to keep her too," Anthony says quietly. "Which means she needs to know who she's standing near."

Lucien nods. "She should know who we are and what our family is capable of...while she may not need to know recent events, the past certainly should be discussed."

Enough to keep her alive.

Enough to keep her away from the Romeros.

Enough that she can choose me with open eyes — or not at all.

No. Not an option.

Alex laughs across the bar, loud and easy. Some random guy sits his hand possessively against Isabella's back. Anthony stills at my side, and I note his attention is on the small group as well—one of them in particular.

My jaw locks. There is definitely history there, and it's not something we need. The further we can get from that family, the better.

I hear Alex mention Dallen to the man who's joined them, his words clear to hear across the space. Deliberate provocation. Do these Romeros never learn when to fuck the hell off?

If he wants my attention, I'll give it to him.

I push back from the table slowly, the scrape of my

chair sharp against the floor. The sound of the bar dims around me, the smell of beer and food thick in the air. My focus narrows to a single point of order.

Alex Romero.

"Stephen, sit down," my brother says. I ignore him.

Alex is standing now, drink in hand, eyes bright with challenge as he watches me move toward him. His sister lingers just behind, watching with too much interest, like she knows exactly how this ends and wants a front-row seat.

"Careful, Moretti," Alex says smoothly as I approach. "You look tense. Wouldn't want you doing something you regret."

I stop close enough to smell the whiskey on his breath. "You already crossed that line when you mentioned Dallen in your conversation. You don't get to speak her name. Ever."

His smile sharpens. "Did I? Or are you just upset I have a front-row seat to your pretty girl? And boy, is she a pretty one. Very soft-looking skin. I'd hate for anything to happen to such a perfect complexion."

My fists curl at my sides. I think of Dallen. Her laugh. The way she stiffens when she thinks she's losing control of a situation. The way she trusts systems that put men like Alex, like me, away forever. She can't be involved, and yet I'm too much of a selfish prick to let her go.

Only I can keep her safe. No one will touch her if I'm around.

"You go anywhere near her again," I say quietly, "and I'll bury you so deep not even cadaver dogs will be able to sniff out your rotting body." The thought of Dallen maimed, broken, and a shell of who she used to be at the hands of the Romeros spurs a fury in me that I see nothing but red.

Alex chuckles. "Touchy." He leans closer, voice dropping. "She's a smart little lawyer, too. Not shrewd enough to keep away from you or work for people who might get her hurt. But then, Romeros and Morettis are no strangers to danger. If she is going to be part of your world, maybe she should learn early what to expect."

That's it.

I don't think. I don't plan.

I move.

My fist connects with his jaw in a clean, brutal arc. The crack is loud enough to cut through the music. Alex staggers back into a table, bottles crashing to the floor as patrons shout and scatter.

Someone yells.

Someone else laughs nervously.

I'm on him before he can recover, grabbing his jacket and slamming him into the bar. Wood splinters under the impact. He swings wildly, catching my shoulder, but it barely registers.

All I see is red.

All I feel is the cold certainty that he meant every word.

I drive my knee into his gut. He grunts, folding, and I use the opening to smash his head back against the bar top. Glass shatters—blood spills.

The bouncer starts toward us, but Lucien steps in front of him, calm as sin. Anthony's already moving too, keeping the sister back, murmuring something sharp in her ear.

Alex claws at me, desperation creeping into his eyes now. "You think you've won?" he spits, blood on his teeth. "You think this ends anything?"

I lean in close, my voice low and lethal. "This ends *your* testing me."

I hit him once more for good measure and let him drop.

The bar is chaos now. Chairs overturned. Drinks spilled. The music stutters, then cuts entirely, leaving only the hum of voices and the sharp ring in my ears.

Alex scrambles to his feet, fury replacing shock. He points at me, wild-eyed. "This isn't over, Moretti." His gaze flicks past me — toward where he knows Dallen exists in my world. "You and your whore girlfriend are going to regret this."

The word snaps something in me.

Lucien steps forward, a dangerous smile in place.

"Careful," he warns. "You're already leaving with your pride in pieces. Don't make it worse."

Alex laughs again, but it's hollow. He backs away, his sister pulling him toward the door. "Tell your girl to watch her back," he calls. "She's playing in waters she doesn't understand."

Then he's gone.

The door slams behind them, the echo loud in the sudden quiet.

I stand there for a moment, chest heaving, knuckles throbbing, blood not all mine streaking my hand.

Dallen's face flashes in my mind again. Fear claws at my gut this time — sharp and unwelcome. They've said her name out loud now, which means this isn't just business anymore. It's personal.

And I'll burn the world down before I let them touch her and burn them in it.

EIGHTEEN

DALLEN

I TELL MYSELF I DESERVE A DRINK. NOT BECAUSE I've had a hard day at work—though I have—but because my head won't shut up. Because every quiet moment is filled with Stephen. His mouth, his hands, his sweetness and temper, the way he looks at me like I'm something he's already decided belongs to him. And because if I don't talk this shit out with someone sane, someone who knows me beyond the lawyer and the good daughter and the woman who always does the right thing, I might actually implode.

I text Amy and tell her to meet me at the bar near my office—the one with the low lighting, the decent cocktails, and the merciful anonymity of weekday crowds. By the time I arrive, heels clicking against worn floorboards, the bar hums softly, glasses clinking, muted laughter rising and falling like background noise. It smells like citrus, gin, and polished wood. Familiar. Safe.

Amy is already there, perched on a stool with a martini in hand, dark hair loose around her shoulders. She smiles the moment she sees me. "There she is," she says. "You look like you're either about to cry or commit a felony."

I snort as I slide onto the stool beside her. "Both are still on the table."

She signals the bartender. "Dirty martini for the woman clearly in emotional distress."

I wrap my fingers around the cool glass when it arrives and take a sip, letting the burn settle me. "Okay," she says, turning fully toward me. "Talk."

I open my mouth, then close it again. Where do I even start? With Stephen and his possessive intensity? With my parents and their quiet disapproval that presses in on me like a vise? With the fact that I'm representing men whose names now make my stomach knot?

"I'm seeing someone," I say finally.

Her eyebrows shoot up. "Seeing someone, or *seeing* someone?"

"*Seeing* someone," I admit. "Sort of. It's complicated."

She grins. "When isn't it?"

I take another sip, buying time. "His name is

Stephen, the hot god I met at the club a couple of weeks ago."

Her expression sharpens with interest. "Okay, wow, wasn't expecting that." She studies me a moment. "So, what's the catch?"

"There are several," I say. "He's intense. Infuriating. Completely inappropriate for both my family and my work, and probably me too."

"And?"

"And I can't stop thinking about him." Wanting him. Wanting to be near him, have him next to me in bed, or walking down the street, enjoying simple quiet time. Urgh! I'm so pathetic.

Before she can respond, a man wraps his arm about my shoulder and squeezes. I look up, expecting to see a friend, someone I know. My stomach drops at the sight of Elio, suit jacket slung casually over his shoulder, untrustworthy smile already in place—too easy, too familiar.

"Well," he says, "if it isn't my favorite lawyer."

My spine stiffens. "Good evening." I wiggle out of his hold, and he thankfully gets the hint. Amy raises her brow at his familiarity but remains quiet.

He leans an elbow on the bar, far too close for my liking. "Didn't expect to see you here."

"I work nearby," I reply coolly. "And I'm meeting a friend...is there anything I can help you with?"

He chuckles, eyes flicking to Amy, then back to me. "Lucky me."

"Well, have a good evening, Mr. Romero," I say pointedly, wanting him to leave. Outside of work, I have nothing to discuss with this man, something he's fully aware of. Stephen's warning rings loud in my mind, and I can't help but feel he's up to something.

"Business, business," he waves off. "Always so serious. Fortunately, we've met here. Maybe we can have a drink?"

His hand lands on my lower back. Not aggressive—but deliberate. Claiming. I step away immediately. "Please don't touch me, Mr. Romero."

He laughs like I'm joking. Amy stands and glares at him. "Relax. I'm just being friendly." He raises his hands in defeat, but it's clear he isn't just friendly. Slimy, yes. Friendly? Hell no.

"No," Amy cuts in sharply. "You're being a slime. Back off."

He doesn't even look at her, and unease slides down my spine, slow and cold. I've dealt with entitled men before, but the way he ignores Amy entirely makes the hairs on the back of my neck prickle.

"I need to speak to you privately," he says to me, lowering his voice. "Just for a minute."

"There's nothing we need to discuss outside of

work," I reply. "This is inappropriate, Mr. Romero. You need to walk away now."

He leans closer anyway. "Come on. Don't make a scene."

I don't want attention. I don't want drama. And some stupid part of me thinks if I placate him for thirty seconds, he'll leave. "I'll be right back," I murmur to Amy, already hating myself.

He guides me toward a quieter corner near the hallway, where the music is duller, replaced by the hum of an air conditioner vent and muffled voices. "This is inappropriate," I say again as soon as we're out of earshot. "You need to leave me alone when I'm not on company time." Not that I'll have to see the Romeros soon, since my boss has agreed to take them on as clients so that I can step away.

He grins—and lifts his phone and quickly dives in next to me. Far too cozy looking and now captured in an image. The camera clicks before I can react.

"What the hell was that?" I snap, pushing him away.

"Just a photo," he says, chuckling lightly. "You look good tonight, Dallen."

Fury burns away my fear. "Miss Byrne to you and you will not take photos of me. You will not touch me. And you will not contact me again. Do you understand?"

His smile doesn't falter. "Careful," he murmurs. "You don't want to upset the wrong people."

A chill runs down my spine, and my denial of what both Stephen and my father have said to me shames me. "I'm done. Go away."

He steps back, hands raised in mock surrender, but I know—deep in my gut—that isn't harmless flirting. It's a warning.

When I return to Amy, she takes one look at my face and slides off her stool. "What did he do?"

I tell her everything. What Stephen has said about the family, what my father disclosed just this morning in my office. About the photo, his dismissal of personal space. The threatening tone and words. My skin crawls at the thought of ever seeing the Romeros again. I tell her about Stephen, his family, and what I've found online about them. I tell her everything, spilling my truths out like verbal vomit.

Amy listens silently, jaw tight. "Your father was right," she says finally. "And so was Stephen."

I sigh, my heart at odds with my commonsense brain. I should remove myself from all of this drama. I don't need to get involved with a family that has so much baggage. Why couldn't I find a nice, hot guy who didn't have danger tattooed on their body like Stephen clearly does?

But even thinking of seeing anyone else, of moving

on, my heart seizes. To not see Stephen again. To not
have him own me, kiss me with his wicked mouth, to
have him shelter me with his chiseled body, I loathe the
thought.

Maybe there's something wrong with me wanting
the bad boy? But is he so bad? He's a property investor
and his family's real estate agent. How wicked could he
be? Just because his family had a history of being in the
underworld doesn't mean they are now.

Before I can respond, my phone buzzes. Once.
Twice. Three times. Stephen. With an image
attachment.

My fingers tremble as I open it. The selfie of Elio
and me. Close enough to look intimate. My heart slams
against my ribs.

> Where are you? Why is he with you?

"Oh God," I whisper.

"What?" Amy asks, leaning over to look at my
message. Her eyes widen. "Oh no."

"I have to go. I'll call you tomorrow." I kiss her
cheek and head for the door.

"Be safe," I hear Amy call from the bar.

I leave in a rush, the cab ride stretching my nerves
thin. When I arrive before Stephen's building, I'm
already bracing myself. He buzzes me in, his tone calm,

but I know he's fuming. I would be, too, if the roles were reversed. Even after knowing him for such a short amount of time, I know I'd hate to see him with another woman. Even if caught in an innocent trap, as the one I was tonight.

The elevator doors slide open—and Stephen is standing in his apartment's foyer, waiting.

The moment I see his bruised face, bloody knuckles, and barely restrained anger, my breath catches. "What happened to you?" I whisper.

The doors close behind me.

And I know—absolutely—that tonight is far from over.

NINETEEN

STEPHEN

I SEE IT THE SECOND THE LIFT DOORS OPEN—THE hesitation in her step, the way her eyes flick up and lock onto my face before she can stop herself. Shock lands first. Then concern. Then something far more dangerous.

Pity.

I hate that one most of all.

"Stephen..." Her voice softens, the word catching like she isn't sure whether she's allowed to say my name anymore. "What happened to you?"

"Nothing of importance." I step back to give her more space, my body tight with the effort not to reach for her, not to pull her into me, and remind myself she's still mine.

The foyer of my apartment is quiet, the muted

hum of the city seeping through a window, and it feels like the calm before the storm.

I turn and move into the apartment, not waiting for her to follow. I hear her soft footsteps that stop when she makes it just inside the doorway, her attention drifting to my cut-up hands, a slight frown marring her perfect brow.

"What happened to you?" she asks.

I don't answer. I shut the foyer door, the sound loud in the silent apartment. The image is still burned into my brain—her face tilted toward that Romero bastard, his arm about her shoulders, his gleeful smirk that tells me he knows exactly what he's doing. I feel it then, that snap inside my chest, the same one that's been with me my whole life. The one that says if someone threatens what's mine, dares to touch what doesn't belong to them, they don't get a second warning.

"I'm fine," I say eventually, stripping my jacket off and tossing it aside.

"You're not," she replies, sharper now. "Your jaw is bruised—"

Well, no fight is fair if one punch doesn't land on me. "I said I'm fine."

She doesn't flinch at my tone, but I see the way her shoulders tense. I hate that I did that. I hate even more that part of me wants to pace, wants to burn this feeling out of my system with violence, the way I was taught. It takes effort—real effort—to stay still.

To not let the fury burning within me take hold.

She crosses her arms. "Then talk to me."

I laugh once, short and bitter. "Talk then?" I cross my arms. "Do you enjoy your little photo shoot with Elio? Quite the friendship considering you're their lawyer."

Her jaw tightens, and as if sensing a forthcoming argument, she too crosses her arms. "He sprung it on me without my consent. There was nothing more in it than that."

"He isn't being friendly," I continue, my voice low. "He's marking territory. Romeros like to do that. You should ask Lucien's wife how well that went for her when she married into that family." My laugh is low and lacks amusement. "Elio is showing me he can get close to you whenever he wants and that you let him." Possibly a low blow, but my temper can't hold back the observation.

Her eyes flash. "He didn't get close because I wanted him to."

That should be enough. It isn't. The fear gnaws anyway, sharp and relentless, because I know how men like Elio think. I know how my father would have thought. And God help me, I know how I've thought in the past when something precious is put in front of me like bait, and I can use it to hurt another.

"You should've told me you were meeting someone tonight," I say.

Her head snaps up. "Excuse me?" she scoffs. "I don't have to tell you what I'm doing every minute of every day. We're not exclusive, and even then I can do whatever the hell I want."

There it is—the steel under the silk. The woman who won't be told what to do, even when the danger is real. I respect it. I want to cage it. Both truths exist, and that terrifies me.

"You don't get to police me," she continues. "Not my job. Not my movements. Not my life."

I scrub a hand down my face, the ache in my jaw grounding me. "That's not what I'm trying to do, damn it."

"It feels like it."

I don't deny it, because lying won't help. Perhaps I am trying to cage her, but with my past, my family, and the enemies who continue to circle our family like sharks, what the hell does she expect? "I'm trying to keep you alive."

Her expression shifts, uncertainty flickering through her anger. "That's a bit dramatic, don't you think? While I understand, perhaps better after today, what you've been trying to tell me regarding the

Romeros, I doubt they're going to kill me just to get at you. I'm not anything special."

"You're special to me," I admit. Her eyes widen at my words, but I won't take them back. They're true, I do care for her, more than anyone else ever, and why shouldn't she know that? Why shouldn't she know that I'd do anything to keep her safe?

"Those men don't play by society's rules, Dallen. They don't care about boundaries, professionalism, or what's appropriate. They care about leverage and revenge, and they think they have a score to settle with the Morettis."

She hesitates, and I see the crack in her certainty. "I dropped them," she says quietly. "As clients. My boss is taking them on, so I'll not be working with them anymore, not after what I found out earlier today from some intelligence from my father's office."

The words hit harder than I expect. Relief slams into my chest, followed immediately by something colder—annoyance. Because it isn't enough to trust my words, she needs to hear the truth from someone she trusts absolutely.

Her father...

"Glad to hear it," I say.

"Thought you might be." She lifts her chin, pride and fear warring in her eyes. "My father told me of some intelligence which he believes could place me in danger. That I'm dating you doesn't help matters, and he's asked me to end things between us as well. Not that we've really started anything. Fuck buddies isn't too deep, is it?"

My stomach tightens, and I ignore her jab at our relationship status and home in on what her father divulged. "What did your father tell you?"

Her breath stutters. "That they're using me to possibly aggravate the Morettis, which seems to be working in their favor. That they're using the guise of needing a lawyer to use me against you, possibly. I mean, I don't know what these people are capable of. I can only imagine the worst, given the family's history, but I don't want to get involved or mixed up in any of it. I had a brother who died a couple of years ago, shot in the crossfire of gang violence, warring groups." She pauses. "I have a great job that I will not jeopardize."

"You had a brother?" *Shit.* That's new information and not something I can dismiss. That her family have lost loved ones to crime doesn't make my pursuing of Dallen any easier. If anything, it makes it harder. In a way, I can't blame her parents for wanting me gone.

She nods. "I'm all they have left."

I take a calming breath at hearing the everything I've been dreading. The bridge between our worlds is collapsing under the weight of truth and history.

Under the weight of what being involved with a Moretti brings to someone's life.

"And me?" I ask, even though I already know. "Are you going to do what Daddy says?"

Her silence is answer enough.

"He told me to stop seeing you," she says eventually. "I've worked so hard for everything I have. I don't know how to navigate this path." She pauses, meeting my eyes. "It's not a secret I want you, but I don't know if that's enough."

The words land like a blade, slicing clean and precise. I don't react outwardly, but inside, something coils tight, feral and furious. Losing deals, losing territory, losing men—I've survived all of it. Losing her? I don't know how to live with that.

"So, what are you going to do?" I ask. "Be a good or bad girl?"

She looks at me then, really looks at me, like she's trying to decide whether I'm worth the risk of everything she's been taught to believe. Debating whether my provocation is enough to make her walk away. She should walk away. Her life would be better for it. Safer.

But she's not going anywhere, no matter what she decides. I'll force her to see reason before I allow anyone, any fear, past or present to make her to step away from me.

"I don't know," she admits. "I don't know who you really are."

The fear claws at me then—not fear of exposure, not fear of consequences, but fear that the truth will finally cost me something I can't replace. Lucien stated she needs to know the truth of the family and allow herself to decide. I grind my teeth, bracing myself to reveal a part of my world that, other than blood, no one knows of.

"What do you want to know?" I ask.

"Everything," she counters. "I know what you choose to tell me. I know what the internet says, what the Romeros think, and I know what my father's seen in thirty years on the force, what he's advising me to do now. But I want to hear it from you. I want the truth of your life, both past and present."

I nod slowly. "That's a lot to take in. Are you sure you're ready to hear without judgment? You're a lawyer after all."

Her eyes search my face. "I need to know before I can make any decision in my life."

I hesitate. I've faced judges, enemies, men with guns and grudges, but this—this feels like standing on the edge of a cliff and deciding whether to jump.

I hate heights.

"My father was a killer," I say. "And up to a point in my life, the eldest three boys in the family, myself included, had dealings in the underworld that are not legal." A nicer way to say that I've killed without coming straight out and saying I've shot people in the head, buried them where they'll never be found, or dumped them far out at sea.

Nothing I'm proud of, but also when one wants to survive, to kill or be killed, one does what's needed. Lucien tried to shield us, and I do believe he thought he'd succeeded, but our father was a crafty old bastard, and there was a lot Lucien was utterly unaware of.

Dallen stills.

"Not rumors. Not exaggeration," I continue. "My father was mafia personified, through and through. He built his reputation on spilling blood, preferably not his own."

Her hands lift, as if she doesn't quite know what to do with them, then drops them at her sides. "And you?"

The question is quiet. Dangerous.

"I've done things I'm not proud of," I admit. "Things I won't soften for you. You're an intelligent woman. I'm certain you can fill in the blanks."

Tears gather in her eyes, and it guts me. I want to pull her close, shield her from the ugliness of it, but she deserves honesty, not comfort.

"That goes against everything I believe in," she whispers.

"I know."

"I grew up with law and order," she continues, voice shaking. "With the belief that men like your father destroy everything they touch. That they deserve to pay for their crimes, not make money off it."

"And men like me spend their lives trying to clean up the wreckage," I say. "We have tried as a family to move on from our shady past, but it continually tries to pull us back. With the death of Matteo Romero last year, that family believes we had a hand in it because Lucien married Matteo's ex-wife."

"And did you?" She studies me, pain and confusion etched across her face. "Your brother—Lucien. Was he involved?"

I don't answer fast enough, and how could I? He did kill Matteo, and he would do it again in a heartbeat.

Her breath catches. "So he is guilty."

"We protect our own," I say carefully. "That hasn't changed, and nor will it ever. Any family would do whatever they could to keep those they love alive."

"And that protection includes murder?" she asks, horrified. "You cannot be serious?"

"If someone threatens my family?" My jaw tightens. "Yes, it includes elimination of the problem."

The silence stretches, heavy and suffocating. I can see she's trying to reconcile the man she thinks I am against the one I'm stating I can be. Of what I'm capable of.

"You expect me to accept that?" she asks. "Even knowing that Lucien Moretti killed Matteo Romero should be something I report. I took an oath."

"No," I say quietly. "I expect you to decide if you can live with it, but what I tell you here and now goes no further."

She laughs softly, broken. "That's not fair." She starts to pace. "And if I don't do as you ask? Are you going to shoot me in the back of the head, too? Shut me up?"

I stare at her, unable to believe she'd say such a stupid thing. "Of course not, and while I know nothing I say about my past is easy," I reply. "I won't lie to keep you. You deserve to know who you're seeing."

She wipes her cheeks, and I clock that she's silently crying. "I can't see you anymore, Stephen. This is too much."

"You're not going anywhere," I say, even though part of me hates that I'm being so controlling and not allowing her to have her independence. But I don't want to lose her either. We interlock perfectly in all ways, and I'll be damned if I allow anything to come between us.

I have to keep her safe, keep her close, keep her out of reach of men who would hurt her to get to my family. Wanting and owning are different things—but I was raised in a world that never taught the difference.

That life lesson is hard to break.

"I'm scared," she admits. "You have to let me go so I remain out of harm's way, surely you see that."

The confession punches straight through my chest. "It doesn't matter now. It's too late. They know I care about you, and whether we're together or not, they'll seek you out."

Her brows knit together. "But you said your family is clean now. They have no proof that Lucien killed Matteo, so why the obsession with justice for revenge? It doesn't make sense how they can blindly go after your family without any evidence."

"They don't need evidence. They have hatred, and they're not stupid. My brother was careful, exact with what he did. They didn't have the evidence to pin it on him, but anyone with half a brain cell knows what the Morettis did," I say.

She exhales shakily. "So either way, I'm a dead person?"

I step closer, stopping just short of touching her. Every instinct in me screams to grab her, hold her, show her she'll never be dead, not on my watch, but I don't. Because if I do, there will be no turning back. "I'll never allow that to happen. Ever."

Her eyes shine with unshed tears, and for a moment neither of us speaks. The city hums outside, indifferent to the war being fought inside my apartment, my chest. I stay where I am long after she stops speaking, after the air between us grows heavy with everything disclosed and yet to be said.

I don't touch her. I don't move. Because if I do, I don't trust myself to stop at restraint. Every instinct I was raised with tells me to pull her close, to decide for her, to remove the threat and the doubt and the people who think they get a say in what's mine. That instinct has kept me alive more times than I can count. It's also the very thing that could cost me her.

She stands there, shaking but unbroken, and it hits me with brutal clarity that Dallen Byrne is not like the women who've passed through my life. She won't bend just because I want her to. She won't stay out of fear, lust, or convenience. If she stays, it will be because she chooses me—knowing precisely what that choice costs. And the terrifying part is that I don't know if I'm strong enough to survive it if she doesn't.

I tell myself I could walk away. That this would be easier if I did. That men like me aren't meant to have nice things, good things, things that can be ruined simply by standing too close to. But the lie doesn't hold. It never has. I've built empires from rubble. I've buried monsters and become one when I had to. I don't quit. Not on deals. Not on enemies. And not on the woman who makes me want something more than survival.

The Romeros won't stop. I know that as surely as I

know my own name. They tasted leverage tonight, and men like them don't forget that flavor. If they think Dallen is a weakness, they will circle. Prod. Push. And I will end them before I let that happen, whether she understands it or not. That truth settles into my bones, cold and absolute.

I look at her again—this woman who believes in rules and justice and a world that plays fair—and wonder how long it will take before she realizes she's already stepped into my shadows. Before she understands that loving me means danger, whether she wants it or not.

And still, knowing all of that, I want her, wouldn't change the past if I were to meet her anew.

I want her standing in my space, challenging me, refusing to bow. I want the fire, the conflict, and the impossible pull between us. I want the woman who makes me fear loss more than death.

If she walks away, I will follow.

But if she stays?

God help anyone who tries to take her from me. "You're mine. I love you." The words spill from me before I can pull them back. I let her know everything tonight. I'll either live or die by my sword.

TWENTY

DALLEN

I DON'T SPEAK FOR SEVERAL SECONDS AFTER Stephen says the three words I'm not expecting.

He loves me.

Holy shit.

The words don't echo so much as they detonate, scattering everything I think I understand about us, about him, about myself.

I'm in love with you.

They sit between us, heavy and exposed, impossible to take back, impossible to ignore. My chest tightens, not with panic exactly, but with something far more dangerous—want. Not simply for his body, not just for the heat and the way he looks at me like I'm the only thing mooring him to the world, but for the certainty in his voice. The way he says it is like it's already decided, like loving me is a fact rather than a choice. Or perhaps it's both.

And that terrifies me.

I drag in a breath that feels too shallow, my pulse loud in my ears, my heart tripping over itself as I try to make sense of the man in front of me. This is the same Stephen who just calmly admitted his family has killed to protect their own. The same Stephen whose brother murdered a man and walked free. The same Stephen who says he'd do it again if someone threatens the people he loves. And now he's telling me he loves me, like it's a gift instead of a loaded weapon.

"I don't..." My voice cracks, and I stop, pressing my lips together as I try again. "Stephen, I don't know what to do with that." And I don't. I'm not sure of anything right now. My mind is a kaleidoscope of thoughts, swirling into one giant mess.

He doesn't move. He doesn't reach for me. He watches, eyes dark and intent, like he's bracing for impact. That restraint makes it worse. If he touched me right now, I might fold. Might let the fear dissolve into something simpler, something physical. But he doesn't, and I'm left standing in the wreckage of my own thoughts.

But love?

That admission isn't supposed to feel like this. It's supposed to be safe. Familiar. Predictable. Love is supposed to look like my parents—rules and structure and knowing exactly where you stand. It's not supposed to come wrapped in violence and secrets and men who talk about *eliminating problems* like it's a business strategy. And yet, when I look at Stephen, all I can think about is how alive I feel around him, how he sees me, how he doesn't want to soften me or shield me from myself. How he wants me fierce and defiant and standing in his space as if I belong there.

"I don't know if what I feel is love," I admit finally, the truth scraping its way out of me. "I know I want you. I know I don't want to stop seeing you, no matter how everyone around me is telling me to run. But love?" I shake my head slowly. "That feels...too big. Too soon."

Something flickers across his face—disappointment, maybe, or pain—but he doesn't interrupt. He lets me speak, lets me find my footing, and that alone tells me he's comfortable with his admission, no matter how uncomfortable it makes me.

"I've spent my whole life believing in law and order." I start pacing again because standing still feels impossible. I need to move, to work through everything that's being said. "In rules. In consequences. In the idea that no one gets to decide who lives or dies just because they think they're justified. And now you're asking me to reconcile that with the fact that the man I'm sleeping with—" I swallow hard. "—the man I care about, stands outside of all of that at times, and I need to disregard it. That his family defends themselves to the death, not figuratively, but literally."

"I'm not asking you to approve of it or be involved in anything that may happen without your knowledge," he says quietly. "But I do need you to know who you're sleeping next to and what baggage I bring."

"How am I supposed to live with this information and not respond?" I shoot back, facing him. "It's not a small thing to ingest. Your life choices and those of your family are not something I can ignore because the sex is good or because you make me feel something I haven't felt before. Not with anyone..."

He nods, a muscle working on his temple. "I know."

His honesty undoes me more than anyone else's. He's not trying to charm me or talk his way out of it. He's standing in the truth of who he is and letting me decide whether I can survive loving him. And the awful, inconvenient truth is that I don't want to walk away. Every rational part of me says I should. My father's voice echoes in my head, warning me about men like him, about the cost of standing too close to power and violence. Two traits that should never coexist, while another voice—quieter, more insistent—keeps asking me how I'm supposed to give up something that feels this real.

"I'm scared," I admit. "Not just of your family or the Romeros or what any of this could do to my career. I'm scared of how much I want you. Of how easy it would be to let you pull me into your world and damn everything that's come before."

Stephen finally moves, just a step closer, careful, like he's approaching a wild thing. "I don't want to own you," he says, and I almost laugh at the irony given everything he's said and done during our time together. Of course, he wants to own me. He wants me for himself, and I'm pretty sure he'd steal me away from everything I've ever known if he could.

"I want you to choose me. Even if that choice scares you."

I close my eyes for a second, the weight of that settling deep in my chest. Choosing him doesn't just mean choosing a man. It means choosing uncertainty. Risk. A life where danger isn't hypothetical. And yet, when I imagine walking away—going back to clean lines and safe choices and men my parents would approve of—it feels like a lie. Like shrinking myself to fit a version of happiness that's never quite enough.

Like choosing a life without love.

"I don't want to stop seeing you," I say. "Even

knowing everything you've told me. Even knowing what risk your name carries."

He lets out a slow, relieved breath, like he's been holding it. "That's all I need to hear."

"It doesn't mean I accept everything," I add quickly. "It doesn't mean I'm okay with violence or secrecy or being kept in the dark. If this continues—" I gesture between us, "—I need honesty. Real honesty. No half truths."

"You'll get it," he says without hesitation.

"And I need you to try all legal avenues first before you go mad and start acting all mafia on me." I should stop here. Should put distance between us and let my head catch up to my heart. Instead, I feel myself drifting closer, drawn by the heat of him, the gravity he seems to exert without even trying. The tension between us shifts, thickens, turning from sharp edges into something heavier, slower, more dangerous.

"I don't know where this leads," I whisper.

Neither does he. I can see it in his eyes. The fear of losing me wars with something darker, possessive and feral, and for the first time, I understand that loving Stephen means standing right at the edge of that line with him.

He lifts a hand, stopping just short of touching my face, giving me the chance to pull away. I don't. My skin hums where he almost brushes me, my body responding long before my mind can catch up.

I don't know if the madness he makes me feel will ever go away, but right now I know I can't lose what we have. I cannot lose him either.

"I need you to know," I say, my voice barely steady, "that wanting you doesn't mean I'll abandon who I am. I won't stop being a lawyer. I won't stop believing in the law or trying to make you see that my way is the right way to move through life."

"I wouldn't want you to," he murmurs. "I want all of you. Even the parts that challenge me. We all try to be better men, Dallen, but old habits are hard to break. Harder still when some don't play by the rules society lives by."

That's what breaks the last of my resistance. Not the words themselves, but the way he says them, like he understands precisely what he's asking of me and is willing to pay the price. I step into him, closing the space between us, my hands resting against his chest, feeling the steady beat of his heart beneath my palms.

I'm not in love. Not yet. But I know this much with brutal clarity: I'm not walking away.

And when his hands finally settle on my hips, firm and warm and grounding, when his forehead dips to rest against mine, I know I'm choosing danger and choosing desire and choosing a man who could ruin me just as easily as he could protect me.

And I let him.

I WAKE in Stephen's bed, my legs tangled about the sheets. For a moment, I'm not sure where I am, before reality comes crashing down around my shoulders. Not regret—just the weight of knowing I'm crossing a line I can never uncross. I made a choice today, one that I know my parents would disapprove of, and perhaps my old self as well. The girl who follows is gone. I can't live in the past, let fears for the unknown, for possibilities that may never come true, dictate my life. Life is for the living, and I want to see where my relationship with Stephen can go, even if it means stepping into something dangerous, even if it changes me forever.

He's a bad boy with a dark past and possibly a shady future, but one who I know is trying to right the wrongs of his family's history and correct his own urges that lead him astray. And maybe that struggle is what draws me to him most—the effort, the restraint, the cost written all over him. His bloodied hands and bruised jaw from his fight tonight are just one example.

I frown, realizing that I haven't asked him whom he fought. Is it some random guy in a bar or someone he knows? Someone from the world he warns me about? Someone who reminds me how real the danger is?

A knot forms in my stomach, and I turn my head to watch him. He's asleep on his back, one arm lazily lying above his head. He looks so untouchable, and in truth, I don't feel like I have the right to lie next to someone who looks like a god. Or maybe I don't feel worthy of how fiercely he wants me.

Yes, I may be a little hooked on his deadly appearance, but damn, he makes me crave. All. The. Damn. Time. Wanting him feels reckless—and I've never been impetuous before.

I drink in the sight of his chest, his chiseled abdomen, his hip, and lower still. The sheet isn't covering him, and his cock lies flaccid on his leg. I roll onto my side and reach out, running one finger along his dick, watching it as it twitches, even in sleep. This isn't just desire—it's curiosity, power, choice.

Before I can stop myself, I kneel beside him and clasp his manhood. He hardens in my hands, and I stroke him, watching with amazement how much he grows. He's so very clever with his appendage, and oh boy, does he know how to use it... And I want to learn him the way he's learned me.

"Are you going to keep observing my dick or are you going to put that pretty little mouth of yours on me and make me come?"

I jump at Stephen's words, having not realized that he's awake. Heat kisses my chest, and I'm glad for the darkness of the room so he can't see my embarrassment. Or how pleased I am that I do this to him. "Do you want me to put your dick in my mouth?"

I lick my lips, unable to hide my smile when he growls a response. "You know I do."

"Well then, I'd better not disappoint you." I bend down, and for the first time in my life, I suck a man's dick. He's like velvet, yet with a rod of steel that presses down my throat. I suck him, use my tongue to tease while I attempt to pretend to be an expert. I'm not confident—but I'm willing. And that feels just as intoxicating.

"That's it, take all of me. Suck my dick and be a good girl." His fingers tangle into my hair, and he guides me, presses me down. His cock touches the back of my throat, and I try not to gag, but he's so big. And instead of fear, there's trust—complete and reckless.

"Yeah, that's it, baby. Let me fuck your face."

His words make liquid heat pool at my core. I want him, I want to please him. I want him to come in my mouth so I can taste him. I want to belong here, even if I don't know what that costs yet. "Do you like it?" I manage, licking the end of his rod while I wait for an answer.

He growls, his eyes darkening with hunger. "Yes."

I smile. "Good. I aim to please." Not because I have to—but because I choose to.

Without warning, he's up, and before I can protest, he pins me facedown on the bed. He clasps my arm, holding it against my back. With my ass up in the air, he thrusts into me. I scream at his sudden, sweet intrusion. Shock turns instantly into need.

"Stephen," I moan into the sheets as he relentlessly takes me. I feel him come down over me, never once losing his stride. "You like me owning you, taking you, marking you mine."

I can't deny it, not now, not after choosing him. I do like it, the secretive part of me that would never admit to wanting a man—any man—to have so much control, yet I allow Stephen to. Because he doesn't take—I give.

I cannot say why. Lust? Perhaps I am in love with him after all. Maybe I'm deluding myself into believing I'm not when he has already professed to be. Maybe love doesn't arrive gently—it crashes.

"I love you fucking me, yes."

He growls against my ear, and I shiver, the first tremors of my release spiraling through me. "You love more than my cock stretching your sweet, tight pussy."

I close my eyes, fighting not to respond and failing yet again. "I do. I love it. Fuck me. Fuck me hard." Let me forget everything else, just for now.

He gives me what I want, and I come. My orgasm

rips through me, stealing me of my senses, sense of self, and place. I'm lost in the pure bliss he brings me. His thrusts are relentless, prolonging my release.

"Dallen..." He moans my name, his body stilling as he joins me.

We slump onto the bed, lost in each other. Stephen pulls me into his side, kisses the top of my head as I try to gain my breath. His heart thumps loud under my ear, and I listen, hold him close as I allow everything that I know about this man, about myself, to settle around us. Nothing feels simple anymore—but it feels real.

"I'm never letting you go. You're mine now, Dallen."

I kiss his chest and snuggle him tighter. The words should frighten me. Instead, they feel like shelter. "You're mine too."

TWENTY-ONE

STEPHEN

OVER THE NEXT SEVERAL DAYS, WORK KEEPS ME busy, but at night, I get to spend time with the one woman I can't get out of my mind. I fall hard. For the first time in my life, I'm content and determined not to fuck this up.

Content?

Christ. I used to think contentment is weakness—men like me don't get comfortable. We stay sharp. We stay ready. And yet lately, when she's curled against me at night, I feel something dangerously close to peace.

I know she's still struggling with my name, my past, and that of my family, but in time, she'll come to learn that we're trying to do the right things, trying to correct our past wrongs, even if they're for good intentions, keeping those we love safe. I recall my father once saying, "In our world, love and protection are two sides of the same coin. It's your duty to keep your loved ones safe, no matter the cost." His voice echoes in my mind, a reminder of what it means to protect fiercely, a legacy of hard decisions, and the burden of doing what needs to be done.

Just as I'd keep her safe from anyone who dares to take her from me.

And that's the part I can't soften for her. Protection in my world always means force. Finality. She believes in courts and due process. I believe in eliminating threats. Bridging that gap may be the hardest thing I've ever done.

Lucien, accompanied by Anthony, strides into my office. I can see by the slight concern marring their brows that they're worried about something. My guard goes up, and I lean back in my chair, willing to give them my full attention.

The steady rhythm of keyboards outside my office continues, phones ringing intermittently, the muted thud of the copier down the hall. Business hums along like nothing is wrong, like war isn't always one misstep away.

"What?"

They sit and look at each other quickly before

turning back to face me. "We've found out why Alex Romero's sister, Isabella, is back on the scene. She's been bequeathed a large real estate portfolio from Matteo. The building happens to be the Fairbanks building."

"Next door to me here?" What the fuck. I think about that coincidence, and I know it's far from that. "What is she going to do with it?" Nothing in this city happens by accident when a Romero is involved. Property lines are battle lines. Proximity is a strategy.

"Nothing, from what we've found out so far," Anthony states. "Isabella is as crafty and dangerous as any Romero. She'll likely use the building to keep an eye on you and our real estate branch of the business. Or she'll rent it out, which I'm sure is probably the plan. She's an astute businesswoman, much smarter than her family, and its probably why Matteo bequeathed her the building above anyone else. He knows she'd do something with it. While it's not ideal that she's so close, there is little threat for her to be so near at this time."

"Any Romero within a foot of us is never ideal." My words cause Anthony to flinch, and I have to ask, "You were fucking her, weren't you?" I pause. "Don't deny it. There's a history there that Lucien and I picked up on when we saw her at the bar the other week."

"It's long over. I haven't seen her in years," Anthony answers, a muscle in his temple working.

"Doesn't mean there isn't a history and one that could place you at risk," Lucien says. "Would she likely try and reach out, do you think?"

"Unlikely." Anthony shifts in his chair, clearly uncomfortable with the questioning. "It didn't end well."

Nothing ever does with that family. You don't walk away clean. You leave pieces behind. I frown but decide not to push the matter further. Our cousin doesn't want to discuss the Romero chick, and I'll drop the subject—for now.

"How's it going with Dallen? We've not seen you much lately, so I'm assuming everything is going well?" Lucien asks.

I can't stop the smirk that twists my lips. "I'm in love with her. I think she's the one, guys."

Lucien's eyes go wide. Anthony gapes. "Shit, really?" Anthony states, shock resonating in his voice.

"Yeah." I run a hand over my jaw, unable to process the feelings that rise in me whenever I think of Dallen, whenever I'm around her. "She's an amazing woman. So goddamn smart and independent, and she doesn't take any shit—not from me or anyone. While I know she's struggling with her family and their dislike of me, we're having dinner tonight, and I'm hoping to clear the air a bit."

Hoping her father sees the man I'm trying to be, not the one I was or hid when necessary. Hoping she doesn't wake up one morning and decide loving me costs too much.

"Does she know of us?" Lucien asks. "Did you have that talk we discussed?"

I nod. "Yeah, I told her, and she's torn. Clearly, she's a lawyer—how could she not be? But she hasn't run from me yet, so I'm hoping she's working through her fears."

The thought of losing her, of her not being in my life, isn't something I can stomach. I've buried men. I've buried enemies. I don't know how I'd bury what she makes me feel. I don't know how it is that I've fallen so fucking hard, but I have. I won't lose her to anyone. Not her family. Not because of those who hold grudges.

"Where are you going for dinner?"

"Delizioso." Thinking that my restaurant and one Dallen enjoyed dining at might smooth out her parents' nerves. If they knew that I owned the restaurant and if I mentioned my real estate portfolio at some point throughout the meal, they may see that I'm trying to move out of my father's shadow.

If I show them stability. Legitimacy. Growth.

Maybe they see I'm not the ghost of Leo Moretti. If only the Romeros allowed us to.

They are always there, lurking, poking, and trying to start shit that none of us wants. "I'm closing the restaurant, so it's just us. My security card, in case my charm of Dallen's parents doesn't go well, and we'll not have any Romeros popping in, making their presence known." Because if one of them so much as looks at her the wrong way in front of her father, I won't be able to contain myself. And I can't afford that—not when I need the dinner to go well. Everything is riding on the fact that it does.

"Good idea." Lucien narrows his eyes. "So if she's the one, do we need permanent security around her? Anyone connected to us needs it when they're going to be part of this family. An unfortunate perk, but one that's necessary when father's enemies refuse to leave us be."

The word permanent does something to my chest. "I'd appreciate it if you implemented that, yes, and I'll speak to Dallen. Let her know what the deal is. She won't like it, but..." She'll think I'm controlling her again. And maybe I am. But I'd rather have her angry with me than unprotected.

Dead...

"Briar didn't like it either at first. Now Greg, her bodyguard, is her shopping buddy. She has him eating out of her hand, so much so, I sometimes wonder who's looking after who."

I chuckle, knowing that Briar has turned Lucien's world upside down, but in a good way. I want the same with Dallen. I want a future with her, a home, one day a family. A house that doesn't have reinforced glass. A life that doesn't require contingency plans. I don't know if that's possible for me, but I want it with her.

Damn, I have it bad.

"I know we have our issues. Each of us has a history that, at times, is shady and not for public consumption, but I'm going to try to be a better man for her. I know we all need to rectify issues the legal way, and I said I'd try that before anything else, but when it comes to our enemies, the Romeros, it's fucking hard not just to be rid of them without fuss. A challenging habit to break."

"It's not easy." Anthony sighs. "With Matteo's death, they're just waiting to strike at us. They know we did it. Even if they can't prove it, they will strike at us, so be on your guard. The women we love are a sure way for payback. Just remember that."

The women we love.

That sentence settles like a weight on my shoulders. Dallen isn't just a girlfriend. She's leverage. She's vulnerable. And I hand that card to our enemies the moment I let myself fall. The moment they know she's everything to me.

"I will," I say.

"Yeah," Lucien agrees.

My phone buzzes, and I pick it up, warmth flowing through my veins like a balm at the name that pops up.

> I'm going to be held up at work. I've texted my parents to tell them to meet us at the restaurant at eight instead of seven. I'm sorry, but I'll meet you there. X

Just seeing her name eases something in me I didn't realize was tight. I message back.

> Do you want me to come pick you up? I'd prefer to see you before going to dinner.

So I could kiss the shit out of her before meeting her parents. Remind myself that she's mine, that she chose me.

> No, it's fine. I'll be there by eight. Order me a red. I need a large glass after today. X

> Consider it done.

"Everything okay?" Lucien asks.

"Yeah, Dallen is going to be working back an hour, but it's all good. One hour less I have to be with her parents."

Anthony cringes. "I don't envy you, but good luck. Something tells me you'll need it."

Something tells me I will as well. Because charming enemies is easier than convincing a cop that his daughter is safe with a Moretti, and for once, I care how this ends.

TWENTY-TWO

DALLEN

I send off the last email of the day and shut down my laptop. The soft whir of the system powering down seems unnaturally loud in the otherwise quiet office. I lean back in my chair and reach for my phone, sending a quick message to Stephen that I'll be leaving in five.

Tonight is important to both Stephen and me. I have to convince my parents, especially my father, that Stephen Moretti, no matter his family's shady past, is who I want in my life.

By my side.

Did I love him? Had I fallen in love for the very first time?

I sigh and put down my phone, placing several papers into files and setting them neatly in a tray for filing tomorrow. The overhead lights hum faintly above me, casting long shadows across the glass walls of the office. I still don't know. I know what I feel is stronger than anything I've ever felt before. Probably not a hard outcome considering I've not dated anyone seriously, and that Stephen is my first sexual partner.

It's only normal that I would feel far more feelings for him in that case.

Still, my stomach knots thinking about him. I don't want to be apart from him. I plan things with an eye to what he's doing and whether he can be included. I want him at my side, in my bed.

Maybe that means I do love him after all.

"Good evening, Dallen."

I start at the sound of my name. The air in the office feels suddenly thinner. I'm alone, taking the extra hour to get ahead of my workload. The cleaning crew hasn't even come through this floor yet. "Mr. Romero, how did you get in here?"

The pit of my stomach knots, and I stand, glad that the desk is between a man I no longer have any professional relationship with. Why is Elio Romero here? Has security allowed him to come up?

He tips his neck to the side, and I hear it crack in the stillness. "No welcome? No...good evening, Elio, how lovely to see you again? No handshake? Nothing?"

"It's after office hours, and we don't have a working relationship any more than a private one. Why are you here, Mr. Romero?" The smirk on Elio's face raises the hairs on the back of my neck, and I swallow. I force the fear coiling through me down, not wanting him to know his presence here rattles me. That I don't trust him or what he is capable of.

There is something in his eyes that is unnerving...

I know the Romeros are not good people. Granted, they're probably as bad as the Morettis, but at least Stephen's family is trying to right their wrongs. I can't see Stephen cornering any woman in an unoccupied office late at night with unknown motives.

That had to count for something.

Didn't it?

He pulls out a chair and slumps into it. Even from here, the smell of brandy is hard to miss, sharp and sweet in the recycled office air, and I force myself to relax, to think clearly and keep hold of the situation.

"I came to state how disappointed our family is that you're no longer our lawyer. I've come to find out why we've been thrown over to your boss." He pauses, leaning forward on his knees and meeting my eyes. "This decision doesn't have anything to do with Stephen Moretti and you fucking him, does it? That by working for the Romeros put you at odds with the Morettis, who killed my cousin."

I feign ignorance, not wanting to escalate the situation. "I don't know what you're talking about. What I do outside of my position here at Redwood & Tully is my decision, and private at that. Nothing to do with you or anyone else."

"Ahhhh, but you see, Dallen, it does impact us thoroughly, and it pisses us off."

He stands, and I swallow, reaching for my phone and gauging how quickly I need to be to run and reach the emergency exit stairs before he catches me. The elevator will take too long to reach my floor. He'll have hold of me by then.

Sweat beads along my spine, and my heart thumps so loudly in my ears I'm sure he can hear it. I know, without a sliver of doubt, he's going to hurt me. In what way, I don't know, but whatever way it's going to be, it's going to be bad.

Very bad.

"We liked having you work for us. It suited our needs, but now that you no longer wish to, well, we no longer need your services. No longer have use for you."

I clear my throat and smile, even though I know these moments may be the last of my life. The city lights flicker through the window, and the entire office feels like a trap. "Mr. Romero, your family—even if my boss now handles your file—is important to us, and we'll endeavor to ensure you're represented well in whatever legal matters you require. I do apologize for stepping aside, but it was at my senior's request, as he wished to have you on his books. Perhaps if you wish for me to work with you again, I can put forward your disappointment, and we can start fresh first thing next week."

Elio shakes his head, scrunching up his nose. "Nah, I don't think so. We know you chose a Moretti over a Romero, and that's all we need to know about you. But I did want to see you one last time, give you a proper Romero send off."

"A send off?" I'm going to be sick. I know it. "What does that mean?"

I glance at the clock on my desk. Eight twenty. I should be at the restaurant by now. If ever there is a time for Stephen to be concerned, to want to be over-bearing and check on me, now's the time.

As if the thought of him conjures him, my phone lights up, and I can see it's a message from Stephen asking where I am. If I've left yet.

Elio starts to move around the desk, and I do too, wanting to keep the several feet of polished mahogany between us. "It means I'm going to mark you before I hit the Morettis in a way that they'll never dare touch another Romero again."

"Mark me?" I slide toward the door. It's only a few steps away, and open. I can run, but then he'll chase. I slip off my heels, pushing them under the desk while he is distracted, looking over the paperwork scattered there. I remain on tiptoes, not wanting him to know I've taken them off. That I don't trust him.

I'm going to die.

The thought slams around my brain, and I feel detached from my body, like my skin wants to crawl off my bones. Get away from the danger unfolding around me.

"Don't worry. Once it's over, there's no pain. Only peace, or so I've been told."

I stare at Elio, unable to comprehend that someone could be so cruel, so callous, and psychopathic.

Before I can think better of it, I bolt.

I push myself as fast as I can through the office, the carpet burning under my bare feet. I throw chairs over in my wake, anything to make it more difficult for him to catch me. I can hear him, his footsteps pounding fast behind me, his vile, threatening words echoing down the glass-lined corridor and forcing me to run faster than I ever have in my life.

For my life.

I can see the emergency exit sign glowing red at the end of the hall. I'm almost at the door. If I can exit, it'll make it harder for him to catch me. I'm certain it would.

But before I reach the handle, I feel his hand rip against my suit jacket.

I fall face forward, hitting the carpet hard. My

hands burn, my knees too, before he's on me, rolling me over to face him.

His fist slams into my face, and for several seconds, I'm unaware of the pain, of where I am or what's happening, before a second blow drags me back into reality. I reach up, clawing at his face, trying to kick my legs. If I'm going to go down, I'm going down fighting. If it's the last thing I do, I'll put his DNA under my nails so he rots in jail for life.

"You think you're too good for a Romero?" I hear my shirt rip and air kiss my chest. His mouth comes down on my breasts, and he bites. Hard.

I scream, fighting to get away, but he doesn't relent. He's heavier than I think. He grabs my arms, placing them above my head, holding me down with a pressure that tears at my shoulders.

"Let me go. Please don't do this." I'll beg. I'll do anything not to die. To leave my parents. Stephen. The life I've worked so hard to build.

"Shut up, you cunt." He slaps my face, and I'm sure I see stars. I can taste blood, and the adrenaline that has helped me run now makes me feel weak and cold.

His hand reaches between my legs, pushing up my skirt. I sob at his touch, his fingers digging into my flesh, brutal and cruel.

"Please, Elio. Please stop."

"Ohh, yeah, baby. You want this. I know you do." I hear him unzip his pants, his free hand tearing at my clothing.

He lets go of my wrist to adjust himself between my legs, and I take the opportunity to strike. I punch him in the face, and for a moment, I have hope that I may get out of this situation yet. I reach for a desk nearby, trying to anchor myself away, but he's on me again. He clasps my hair and thrashes my head against the floor.

Pain shoots through my skull, and my hands tingle, the fight—or at least the ability to fight—seeping out of me.

I feel him force my skirt up around my hips, my underwear too, and he bends my legs up, placing himself at my core.

I want to vomit.

I want to die and be free of this situation.

I never want to remember this night again.

Death would free me of this nightmare.

He rubs himself against me, and I open my eyes, maybe to say goodbye to the world I knew. The one I loved. The one I would miss.

Forever.

TWENTY-THREE

STEPHEN

THE SMALL TALK IS EXCRUCIATING, AND THERE'S no use pretending that Dallen's parents are going to like me at the end of this dinner. For the past twenty minutes, we've said barely any words, certainly nothing substantial. Dallen will have to make a choice. Me or her family. Not that I'd ever tell her that she can't have both, but when it comes to time with her family, I'll not be present, and she needs to be okay with that. Certainly, her parents will be.

That's the point of Delizioso tonight, even if I know it will fail. Neutral territory. My territory. A quiet, curated space where I can sit across from the Chief of Police and prove I'm not my father. Prove I'm not a headline waiting to happen.

Eight ten comes and goes with stilted conversation and untouched wine. Susan Byrne makes small talk about the restaurant décor. Chief Byrne studies the wine list as if it requires interrogation. I check my phone more times than I want to admit.

Dallen should be here by now.

At eight fifteen, I tell myself she's caught in traffic. By eight twenty, a sick feeling settles in the pit of my stomach. By eight thirty, the lie stops comforting me, and I need to leave.

"Has she texted you?" Susan asks, trying for lightness but failing. There's a tightness around her mouth I haven't seen before, a mother's instinct quietly surfacing.

"Yes. She said she was leaving at five past, but nothing since." I keep my voice steady, but my thumb is already pressing her number again.

It rings.

And rings.

Straight to voicemail. My last message left unread.

Chief Byrne's jaw shifts almost imperceptibly. He tries next. The line fails just as quickly.

"She always answers," Susan says. It isn't an accusation. It's fear creeping in.

"She could be caught in traffic," I reply automatically, though the words feel hollow even to me. Dallen wouldn't ignore my text. She knows what this dinner means. She knows I'm stepping into a room where I'm already judged guilty.

Probably rightfully so, but that's to worry about another time.

I stand, collecting my keys and wallet. "I'm going to head to her office. Make sure everything's okay."

Chief Byrne stands too, neither dramatic nor panicked. Just decisive. "I'll come with you." He turns to Susan. "You head home, just in case Dallen rings or heads there for whatever reason."

We don't speak as we leave the restaurant. We don't debate whether we're overreacting if something could be wrong. But something feels off. An intangible current that runs through a person, intuition, telling you to go, to check, just to be sure...

The drive to Dallen's law firm is suffocating in its normalcy. Traffic lights change. Pedestrians cross. The city moves in ignorant rhythm while something claws up my spine. I try her again. Call. Text. Nothing. Not even left on read.

Where are you, Dallen?

I'm coming, baby.

I pull the car to a sudden stop, not bothering to find a parking spot, merely using the large pedestrian strip out front. The building is lit up, like most NY skyscrapers, but as we head toward the lobby, I can't see the security guard who usually occupies the desk.

I start to run.

We burst through the door, Dallen's father close on

my heels. I skid to a stop as I lean over the desk. That's when I see the guard. He isn't sitting. He's folded awkwardly behind the counter, one arm bent wrong beneath him, blood darkening the side of his head. The sight doesn't register as shock. It registers as confirmation.

Romeros...

Chief Byrne vaults the counter and checks his pulse. "He's alive," he mutters. "Blunt force to the head by the looks of it." He lays him down in a recovery position and picks up his phone. "I'll call 9-1-1, but we need to get up to Dallen's floor."

We take the elevator, the small space enclosing me like a coffin. Each floor passes in heavy silence, broken only by our breathing. The higher we climb, the colder something settles in my chest — not fear exactly, but recognition. This is how leverage works. This is how you send a message.

Light spills into the elevator as the doors open.

And then I hear it.

A scuffle. A chair scraping violently across the floor. A sharp intake of breath that does not belong to someone in control. Pleading.

Dallen begging...

I react, oblivious to who's standing beside me. I don't consider optics, law, or consequences. I bolt down the hall, and the image that meets me will never be erased from my mind, no matter how hard I try.

Dallen is pinned to the floor, her arms trapped above her head in Elio Romero's punishing grip. His naked lower body is positioned against her in a way that needs no explanation. Fury, cold and deadly, rages through me; something ancient and feral snaps free.

I cross the passage in three strides and wrench him off, throwing him several feet from Dallen. I come down on him immediately, drive my fist into his jaw so hard I feel bone give beneath my knuckles. He stumbles to his feet, and I let him, want him upright when I knock him back down. I hear Dallen sob her father's name, her breath hitching as her father comforts her, leaving me to deal with this piece of shit.

Elio laughs. Actually laughs.

"You're going to die tonight," I say.

Blood runs from the corner of his mouth, and he wipes it away like this is a sport. Like he's enjoying the evening. "Told you," he spits. "Romeros always hit back. Pity you were so slow in getting here. You didn't save her at all."

His smirk makes the world before me turn red.

He lunges, but I'm over playing with my prey. I hit him again. And again. We crash into the wall, drywall splintering beneath our weight. He drives his shoulder into my ribs, and we careen into a bookshelf, law journals raining down around us. He's stronger than I remember, quicker, too. He gets a punch in that snaps my head back and fills my mouth with copper.

Pain steadies me.

Grounds me.

Reminds me that this isn't my nightmare. It's his.

He reaches down and comes up with a shard of broken glass from the fallen photo frame. He swings. It slices across my forearm, shallow but sharp enough to sting. That's the moment I stop thinking about consequences. Because if he's willing to use glass, I'm willing to use worse.

I tackle him to the floor, driving him down with enough force to knock the breath from his lungs. My forearm presses into his throat. He claws at my face, my shoulders, my neck. I tighten without remorse.

I can hear Dallen somewhere behind me. I can hear her father telling her to look away.

I can hear my own heartbeat pounding like war drums in my ears.

And beneath it all, another voice.

My father's.

You finish them.

Or they finish you.

Elio's movements become frantic, then uneven. He tries to speak, something about leverage, about how she'll never stay with me after this, about how Daddy won't allow it. The words blur into static.

All I can see is Dallen pressed against the floor. See Elio raping the woman I love and taking what isn't given freely. If I loosen my grip, he'll try again. They never stop. Not these bastards. Every one of them needs to be eliminated.

Something shifts. His resistance weakens. His hands slip.

For a second — one dangerous, eternal second — I realize I'm crossing a line I can't step back from. My hands tighten further.

Chief Byrne's voice cuts through the haze. "Stephen!"

I don't release immediately. I wish I could say I do. I wish I could claim morality reasserts itself. It doesn't. It's exhaustion. It's inevitable. It's the knowledge that the damage is already done.

When I finally pull back, Elio doesn't.

He lies still beneath me, blood pooling darkly beneath his temple where I've struck his head against the floor. Chief Byrne kneels beside me and checks the bastard's vitals. I meet his eyes, his expression one I will never forget — not horror, not anger.

Calculation.

"He's dead," he says quietly.

Dead.

The word lands without drama. Without thunder. Just finality.

Good riddance.

I look back at Dallen. She's shaking, eyes bright with shock and something far more complicated — fear, yes, but not of Elio.

Of me.

And that's the moment the rage leaves entirely. Because killing him was instinct, seeing what it does to her is a consequence. Chief Byrne rises slowly. He doesn't draw a weapon. Doesn't arrest me. Doesn't shout. He looks at me as both father and law.

"You understand what you've done."

I do. And I don't regret it. I'll never regret removing such scum from the world. That realization should terrify me. Instead, what terrifies me is the possibility that Dallen will walk away — not because of rumors, not because of family legacy — but because she's seen exactly what loving me means.

What I'm capable of, even right in front of her and those she loves.

I stand up, hands bloodied, breath still ragged, and I understand with chilling clarity that I've protected her. And in doing so, I may have destroyed any chance of keeping her.

TWENTY-FOUR

STEPHEN

"You should leave via the emergency stairs, get out of the building. I'll take it from here."

The words from Dallen's father halt my steps toward her. "I can't leave. I know what I've done, and I don't regret it. I won't leave her here."

"You will if you love her." The Chief stands, his mouth tight with determination. "Go. I'll be in contact soon."

I turn to Dallen, move to reach for her, but she cowers against the wall. I stop, hate that I've done this to her. That I've placed her in a position that's caused her so much trauma. A trauma no one ever heals from. Not really.

The sight of her shrinking from me guts me worse than any blade ever could. I've killed for her, would kill again without hesitation, and yet I'm the one she recoils from. What does that make me? Savior or monster?

"Dallen..."

"Go," I hear her whisper. "Just go."

A lump forms in my throat, and for several heart-beats I can't move. Will I ever see her again? Is she going to be okay? What can I do to make this better? To make this night disappear? If I could trade places with her, take the memory from her mind and carve it into my own, I would. I would carry it. I would carry all of it.

"Go. The elevator is moving. The cops are here."

I leave the building, exit through the emergency stairs, and make my way to the ground floor before stepping out onto the street through a side door. I shove my hands into my pockets and quickly hail a taxi. I'll go to Lucien's. He'll know what I should do.

My mind isn't thinking clearly, and I don't trust myself to make any sound decisions right at the moment. All I can see is Elio's face under my fists. All I can hear is the crack of bone giving way. And the sick part? The part I don't dare voice? It satisfies something dark in me—something my father would understand perfectly.

I get to Lucien's, and he buzzes me up immediately. His eyes widen at the sight of my face, my hands, as I step into his apartment foyer. Briar gasps and quickly comes toward me, clasping my hand to bring me into the living room.

"What's happened?" they both say at the same time.

I slump into the chair, holding my head in my hands. "I killed Elio Romero tonight. He was..." Goddamn it, how to voice such horror, the memory makes my stomach turn. "Dallen was late to dinner we were having with her parents. She wasn't responding to texts or calls, so her father and I went to her office to check everything was okay. We found Elio there with her." I pause, raising my eyes. They lock with Briar's, and I can see hers are full of tears. "I don't need to tell you what we found."

Her torn blouse. The bruises already forming. The bite on her chest. The sound she made when she saw me—relief and devastation tangled together. I will hear that sound for the rest of my life.

"Fuck." Lucien starts to pace.

Briar comes and sits beside me, places a comforting arm about my back. "Where is Dallen now?" she asks.

"With her father at the office. He called the police and ambulance. I imagine they'll go to the hospital."

"And you just left?" Lucien asks, his tone far from pleased. In fact, it borders on accusatory.

I glare at him, not in the mood for lectures. "No, I didn't leave. The Chief of Police ordered me to go before the cops arrived. I wanted to stay. I know what I did, and I'll face the consequences of it. Goddamn it, I'd do it again, but he ordered me. I don't know why."

And I hate that I obeyed. Every instinct screamed at me to stay, to stand over Romero's body and own what I'd done. Let the world see what happens when someone touches what's mine.

Lucien nods, clearly thinking of everything that could or could not happen from this point. "So we wait. The Chief obviously had his reasons for those orders."

"I don't know what they would be. He loathes me. To pin something like this on me, have front row seats to me expiring Elio's life, is the perfect outcome to keep his daughter out of my hands."

"You love her, don't you?" Briar states, not a question, merely stating a fact.

"I do. When I saw her tonight, on the floor, I can't tell you—the rage that erupted inside of me was beyond reason. Nothing, or anyone, could have changed how this night ended for Romero." It isn't just rage. It's terror. The kind that strips you to bone and leaves nothing but instinct. I thought I was too late. I thought I'd lost her before I'd even had the chance to build a life with her.

"I'm glad he's dead." Briar hugs me tighter.

"You're not helping, sweetheart," Lucien states,

throwing her a reassuring smile. "I'll turn on the news, see if anything is being reported while we wait to hear from Dallen's father. I'm certain we will."

THE CALL COMES LATE the next day. I am ordered to Dallen's parents' house, and I arrive to find the place eerily quiet. I expect cops to come out from behind closed doors and arrest me. I welcome the charge. I don't regret a thing, and I can't be remorseful for removing another Romero from this world.

If prison is the price for keeping her alive, I will pay it. If exile is the cost, I will accept it. What I cannot accept is losing her because I wasn't ruthless enough.

"She's upstairs, first room on the left," her father states when he lets me in. "I'll be in my office. We need to talk before you leave."

I nod and head upstairs, needing to see Dallen as much as I need air. The sight of her on a small lounge in her room, her legs tucked up beneath her, bruising over her face, her lips swollen, her jaw a horrible green and gray color—

My loathing for Elio doubles, and I send up a prayer that I hope he is burning in hell. I should have made it slower. That thought flashes through me before I can stop it. I should have made him feel everything she felt. And that is how I know the darkness in me is not gone—just restrained.

"Dallen?" I knock, not wanting to startle her or come in without permission.

She jumps anyway, but thankfully, upon seeing me, she waves me into her room. "Hi," she says, and my heart crumbles in my chest.

I sit beside her, not sure if I can hold her hand, reach for her, comfort her. I want to, the draw to touch her, to remind myself that she's okay, she's here, alive at least—but I don't. She looks so fragile, so injured and sore. I can't add to her pain.

"I'm sorry." I don't know what else I can say to her. What can I say when it was because of me, because of my family, and our past that brought on this trauma for the one woman I love most in the world?

"I had a choice to leave this relationship, and I didn't. It's not your fault."

She is being too gracious. Too forgiving.

"But it is. I brought you into my world. One that we've been fighting to leave for years, and I knew that. I still pursued you. Refused to think of what could happen... I'm sorry I wasn't there sooner." I will never forgive myself for those lost minutes. For the time it took to act. For the seconds wasted debating whether she was late due to some benign reason. Those seconds could have cost her everything.

She swallows, and I can see the action pains her. "I'm not okay, Stephen, and I need time. I think this has to end until I'm ready. You need to walk away."

I can't walk away. I love her. The thought of not being with her rips open my body, and I clasp my chest, trying to soothe the ache. I've always said I couldn't walk away. That once she was mine, nothing would come between us, not even her family. Every part of me wants to refuse. To say no. To promise vengeance on anyone who dares separate us. But that is the man my father raised. Not the man I want to be for her.

And yet, sitting here, seeing her broken, I can't be the man I was. I can't be another man who takes what's not rightfully given. Freely given. "Okay."

Her eyes widen, as if she expected another response. I don't blame her. I wanted to give a different answer, but I'm not a bastard. A killer, yes. A son of a mafia king, absolutely. But when it comes to Dallen, I'd do whatever she says so that I may have a chance.

A second one that I desperately want.

She reaches for me and hugs me tight. I pull her against me, never wanting to let her go. I breathe in the sweet scent of her hair and kiss her neck, wishing everything could be different. "I'm so sorry I didn't get there sooner, baby." I swear to whatever God is listening, if she gives me another chance, no one will ever touch her again. I will burn the world down before I allow it.

"I'm sorry too."

We hold each other for a long time before she pulls back, settling herself back in her chair. "You should go. I'm feeling tired, and I need to sleep."

I nod and stand, starting for the door. I turn back and drink in the sight of her. Take a mental image of her and what I'll never allow to happen to her again. "I love you, Dallen. I'm sorry."

Tears well in her eyes, and she bites her bottom lip, but doesn't answer.

And why would she? There are no words that can fix this wrong. Correct the past. Only time—and even then, it only ever dulls the ache.

I head downstairs and find Dallen's father in his den. "Close the door," he orders as I step into the room.

I do as he states and take a seat. Now, for my reckoning, which, oddly, will be less painful than saying goodbye to Dallen. "What happens now? I assume you have a warrant for my arrest."

The Chief leans back in his chair and steeples his fingers. "I'm not arresting you. In fact, as far as anyone is concerned, I killed Romero saving my daughter."

I lean forward, not liking that outcome at all. "But there will be footage of me going into the building, of being in the elevator. Of strangling the life from his worthless body."

"There is no footage. Elio Romero had that shut off before he headed up to Dallen's floor. Those bastards are nothing if not thorough."

Anger sweeps through me, and I fight not to lose control of my thoughts. Even in death, they manipulate the board. But they miscalculated one thing—they thought fear and love would weaken us. They were wrong.

"And Dallen and me? What's to happen there?" There was a time when I'd say to hell with her parents. I get what I want, and I want Dallen. She's mine as much as I'm hers, and nothing will keep me from having her. But now? Now everything is changed. She's changed, and I can't disregard her family, her life, as easily as I may have once. I love her too much for that.

"It's no secret I disagree with you seeing my daughter. You're from a family that I'd prefer to take down than align myself with, but my daughter, for whatever crazy, unhinged reason, has fallen in love with you."

The word love steals my breath. "She doesn't love me, Chief. I haven't won that honor." Yet...

"You have," he says, dismissing my denial. "You just haven't heard it, but I'm sure she'll tell you one day. But that you saved her, slayed the monster that will forever haunt her mind, I can't hate you as much as I want. And so if she chooses to see you after she's through this period of her life, then we won't stand in your way. But know this," the Chief states, leaning on the desk and meeting my eyes. "Should you ever hurt her, or anyone ever harms her again because of something you or your family does...I'll hunt you down and shoot you like the dog all you mafia fucks are. I've lost one kid to crime. I won't lose another. Do you understand?"

I fist my hands and release them. I can't throw hands with Dallen's father, no matter how much he's just pissed me off. "I understand."

"Good." He leans back in his chair, his demeanor once again of indifference. "You need to give her time and space. She'll choose when she's ready to see you again, and if she doesn't, you need to be okay with that."

I nod, knowing that the next several weeks, months, years, even, may be the hardest of my life. I reach into my pocket, pull out a note, and slide it across the desk. "If I'm to give her time and not face it, give her my address if she chooses me. I'll be there for the foreseeable future."

The Chief glanced at the address. "Ireland?"

"I have a cottage there. I need some time away from this city. I hope Dallen joins me there. Ireland will help her heal. It'll be good for her." Away from bloodstained hallways. Away from names that carry violence. Somewhere the past can't find us so easily.

"Thanks for keeping my name out of this mess. I didn't mean for any of this to happen when I first met Dallen. I liked her. *I love her.* I want her in my life. Just thought you should know."

The Chief doesn't answer, merely stares at me before I leave. I walk out of Dallen's home and out of her life.

For now.

But I'm not done fighting for her. Not with fists. Not with threats but with patience. With distance. With becoming someone she can choose without fear.

TWENTY-FIVE

DALLEN

Four months later, Ireland

THE FIRST THING I NOTICE WHEN THE CAR TURNS
through the gates is how wrong Stephen was.

Cottage.

Stephen Moretti's "cottage" rises out of the Irish
countryside like something carved from legend—gray
stone walls, tall, mullioned windows catching the pale
afternoon light, ivy climbing confidently toward the
roofline as if it has every intention of claiming the
place. Beyond it, the Atlantic stretches vast and merci-
less, waves crashing against rock in a rhythm that feels
both violent and cleansing.

It's beautiful.

It's imposing.

It's precisely the kind of place a man like Stephen would live.

But cottage? No, it most certainly isn't that.

My pulse hums as the driver brings the car to a stop. I sit there for longer than necessary, fingers tightening around the strap of my bag. I have replayed this arrival in my head a hundred times over the past months—what I would say, how I would stand, whether I would break the moment I saw him.

I am not the same woman who left New York. Not the woman who lay on the carpet of her office, believing she was about to die. But I'm not totally broken either. I've worked hard to repair what I could from that night, and seeing Stephen is my final step to that healing.

I quickly swipe my card and pay the fare, opening the door before I can change my mind.

The cold air hits me—stealing my breath for a moment. I can taste the salt on my lips. It fills my lungs, a sensation that feels almost healing. For so long, everything has smelled like antiseptic, city trash, and fear lodged somewhere deep in my memory. This smells like freedom, security, and possibility.

A new start.

The front door opens before I reach it. Stephen steps out and pauses on the threshold. His gaze devours me. Perhaps a good sign that he hasn't moved on. That I may still ignite something in his heart and mind. But he also looks...different.

Not softer. He will never be soft. But less coiled. His shoulders aren't braced for impact, his jaw isn't set quite so tight. The wildness in him hasn't disappeared —it stirs there beneath the surface—but it's quieter here, like the land itself is absorbing some of it.

We stand there for a moment, looking at each other.

It's been months. Thirteen weeks to be exact, but who's counting?

You were counting, Dallen.

So many weeks of therapy. Weeks of slow, careful conversations with a woman who tells me that trauma does not make me weak. That I shouldn't carry shame as it isn't mine to bear. That no matter what I did, Elio Romero would have attempted what he did to me that night, that it was his choice and his choice alone. That no one blames me, isn't judging me, no matter how much I think they are.

But these past three weeks have been the hardest. Returning to the office three days a week and forcing myself to walk the corridor where it happened. Working at my desk and remembering how everything unfolded.

I survived, and most of that survival lies at this

beautiful man's feet. How I missed him, so much so that some nights I physically hurt.

"You came," he says finally. His voice is steady, but there is something beneath it. Something fragile that I've never heard before.

"I did."

He takes a step toward me and then stops. Is he unsure of himself, or of me? I can't help but think it's the latter.

"Can I hug you?" he asks.

The question alone nearly undoes me. Once upon a time, he would have taken me into his arms, claimed the space, claimed me. The man standing before me now waits for permission.

"Yes," I whisper.

He approaches slowly, arms sliding around me with careful restraint. He doesn't pull me tight. Doesn't crush me against him. He lets me choose the pressure.

I close the space myself, press my cheek against his chest, and relish the feel of his arms around me again. The steady beat of his heart beneath my ear unties something inside me and sends it floating away. Perhaps I also hadn't realized how tightly I'd been holding myself together until this moment.

"I missed you," he murmurs into my hair, kissing

my temple, his warm breath against my ear making me shiver.

"I know." We stand like that for a long time, the wind tugging at us, the sea roaring in the distance, and I realize I'm trembling, not from fear, but from feeling.

Safe...

He draws back enough to look at me. His gaze traces my face carefully, cataloging each of my features. The bruises are long gone, the cuts have healed, the memory too, when I fight hard enough to push it down where it can't control me.

I pray that too dissipates in time.

"You look stronger," he says. "Beautiful as ever."

"I am stronger." It surprises me how easily that truth comes, but it's true.

"Come, we'll sit out the front. There's a beautiful view of the sea that you'll love."

I follow, knowing I'm already in love with Ireland, this house...*him.*

We move around to the terrace that overlooks the cliffs. The stone beneath our feet is cool. The horizon stretches so far it feels like the world could drop away, and it wouldn't matter. New York sits somewhere over that ocean, and for the first time in my life, I wouldn't care if I never saw it again.

We sit side by side. Not touching, just being at first. "I've been in therapy," I tell him. "It's helped me a lot."

He nods. "Your father mentioned it in his last email." He pauses. "I'm glad it's helped. I wanted to be there for you, but I know you needed me to leave. I want you to know that I understand that choice."

"I didn't want to be defined by that night," I continue, my eyes fixed on the waves. "I didn't want to flinch every time someone raised their voice. I didn't want to hate myself for not being stronger. I didn't want to resent you for not listening to me like Elio wouldn't." My throat tightens, and I swallow the lump that's lodged there. "I still have nightmares. Some nights are worse than others. But they're becoming less frequent. I'm back at work three days a week. I walk past that spot on the floor, and I don't see only what happened there. I see that I'm still here and he isn't. I see you, saving me, and it's a comfort I didn't know I needed."

His hand shifts, hovering near mine, but he doesn't reach out. I look at his tattooed hand, so large and strong, heavy with ink, and yet, he's so careful with me. Never punishing, never cruel.

He's the kindest man I know.

"I would kill again to save you," he says quietly.

The bluntness of his words doesn't shock me. Not anymore. There was a time those words would have sent ice through my veins. Now they land differently.

He isn't bragging. He isn't threatening. He is stating a fact.

He would protect his own—those he loved.

"I know," I say. He looks at me then, searching my features, for what I do not know. A lie? Fear? Hesitation?

"I don't admit that lightly," he continues. "I nearly lost myself that night. When I saw him on top of you..." His jaw tightens. "There was a part of me that didn't want to stop. Even after he ceased moving. I wanted to rip his organs from his body. I wanted to throw his worthless carcass from the window and watch it land on the pavement below. I wanted to see his whole family dead."

I remember that look in his eyes. Not just fury. Something darker. Older. "But you did stop," I say gently.

"Barely."

We fall into silence, the wind carrying away the weight of his words. "I've thought about what you did," I admit. "About what it means that you would do that for me."

"And?"

"And I realize something." I draw in a slow breath. "That I'm happy that you killed Elio. I know now that, should I ever be in the situation you were in that night, I too would act the same. I would do anything to protect those I love, no matter the cost. I can't judge you for that."

I turn to face him and clasp his hand. "What happened to me wasn't because of your temper, your family, or your past. It was Elio's choice. His family is seeking revenge on a person who had nothing to do with Matteo Romero's death. They are the cruel ones in all of this. They are the ones who should carry the shame of such actions."

Relief crosses Stephen's face.

"I don't romanticize what you are," I continue. "I don't pretend your family hasn't done terrible things. I'm still a lawyer. I still believe in law and order, and I know what your family has done, by your own admission."

"I know."

"But I also know," I continue. "That the world isn't as simple as I was raised to believe. And that night... You didn't hurt me. You saved me." The words settle between us. "I'm not fully healed," I admit. "Some days I still feel like I'm walking around in someone else's skin. But I didn't come here because I'm fragile. I came because I chose to."

His fingers tighten around mine. "Why?" he asks softly.

Because that's the question. Why would I choose this man, with his shadows and his history and the danger that clings to his name? "I was scared that loving you meant betraying everything I am," I say. "That it meant becoming someone I don't recognize, don't trust, or respect."

"And now?"

"Now I realize loving you doesn't erase my values. It doesn't make me complicit in your past. It means I see you as more than the worst things you've done."

His throat works as he swallows.

"I see the man who asked for permission before he touched me after what happened," I continue. "The man who left when I told him to leave, even though it killed him."

"It did kill me," he says roughly.

"I know." The wind lifts my hair across my face, and he brushes it away, careful, reverent. "I don't know what the future looks like," I admit. "There may be more enemies. More complications. More choices that terrify me."

"There will be," he says without flinching.

"But I don't want to live my life dictated by fear. Not of what happened. Not of what might happen." My heart pounds now, because this is the edge. I'm standing on a cliff about to throw myself into the stormy, choppy seas for the first time in my life. "I love you, Stephen." The words feel enormous. Heavy but real.

His eyes widen, and for a second, he looks almost stunned.

"I love you," I repeat, my voice steadier. "Not because you saved me. Not because trauma bound us together. But because I chose you. Knowing who you are. Knowing what you're capable of. Knowing all of your past. I choose you."

His swallow is almost audible.

"I am not naïve," I continue. "I know you would kill again if someone threatened me. Part of me always knew that. It doesn't scare me the way it used to. I would kill for you, too. For the family I hope we make one day."

He searches my face. "Family?"

I nod. "Yes, our family, the one we create together." The sea crashes below, relentless and alive. "I don't need you to be perfect. I need you to be honest. To try the lawful way first before moving into any other direction." I grin. "To let me stand beside you, not behind you like some precious porcelain doll."

"You will never stand behind me," he says firmly. "Never."

Emotion swells in my chest so sharply it hurts. "I don't want to lose myself again," I whisper. "I don't want to lose you either."

"You won't lose yourself with me," he says. "And I won't lose you without a fight."

A small, watery laugh escapes me. "That I know."

He pulls me gently toward him, and this time I go fiercely, resting my forehead against his. "I love you." The words are a low, guttural growl. "And whatever comes next—your healing, my past, our families—we face it together."

Together.

The word settles into my bones. For months, I've been rebuilding myself piece by piece. Reclaiming my body. My mind. My autonomy. And sitting here, on a cliff overlooking a sea that looks wild enough to swallow the world, I realize something else.

What happened to me does not end me.

It does not steal my future.

And loving him does not make me weak.

It makes me brave.

"I love you," I say again, just to feel how wonderful it is to admit those words aloud, to make them real.

He kisses me then—not desperate, not claiming, but slow and deliberate seduction that leaves me breathless—a promise instead of a demand.

The wind howls around us, and for the first time in a long time, the future doesn't feel like something to fear. It feels like something to step into.

With him.

EPILOGUE

DALLEN

One Year Later, somewhere over the Atlantic Ocean

"STOP STARING AT ME LIKE THAT. I'M NOT BEING naughty with you 30,000 feet in the air." I can't help but laugh at Stephen and his inability to behave, even in front of his family who are all on this jet with us. They're heading to Ireland, to see where Stephen and I are making a home.

A permanent home after everything that happened in New York. Thankfully, my work allows me to work remotely for the moment, even though I do jet back and forth across the Atlantic when needed. This time away from the city is healing.

The hum of the engines is low and powerful, a steady reminder that we are suspended over an ocean, wrapped in steel and luxury and second chances. The cream leather seats, polished walnut trim, and soft recessed lighting make it feel less like an aircraft and more like a private lounge drifting through the sky. A far cry from the chaos we left behind in New York.

There are still nights when I wake and expect sirens, flashing lights, or the cold press of fear in my chest. Ireland gives me quiet. Gives me space to breathe without looking over my shoulder.

Ireland is healing.

Stephen too.

I see it in him—the way his shoulders no longer sit so rigid, the way his laughter comes easier now. But there are shadows in him that will never entirely disappear. I understand that. I carry my own.

I adore him.

Even if right at the moment he's trying to convince me to join an absurd club I refuse to be part of. "No," I say again.

He grins, that devilish, tempting smirk that I struggle to deny. I rarely do. I'm kind of addicted to the guy, and I love him. Still, with all his family around, I can't possibly do what he wants.

The cabin stretches long and sleek behind us, divided into zones of plush seating and a dining area with crystal, neatly secured in cabinets. Billionaire indulgence. Every detail curated. Every surface gleaming. And yet all I can focus on is the heat in his eyes.

He leans forward, his biceps flexing and catching my eye. I reach out and run my hand along one of the snake tattoos. "You know you want to. I can almost smell your desire for me, Pumpkin." His voice drops low, intimate, cutting through the jet's refined elegance like something deliciously inappropriate.

"Don't lie to me and stop teasing." I chuckle when he runs his hand along my thigh, tightening his hold and tickling me. "You're not playing fair."

"I never play fair." He comes and sits beside me, and I watch as he looks behind our seats. "No one is taking any notice of us. We could go to the bathroom at different times. It'll be fine." His whispered words against my neck make me shiver, the soft, beckoning kiss afterward has me seriously considering doing what he wants.

A year ago, I wasn't sure we'd even have this—this teasing normalcy, this reckless happiness. The thought of losing him back then still makes my stomach knot.

"I'll die of embarrassment if any of them suspect. We only have a couple of hours before we land. I'm sure you can wait until then to get your rocks off."

He shakes his head, serious all of a sudden. "No, I can't. I'll expire of need if I have to wait to have you. I want you, and here, feel this." He clasps my hand and places it on his lap.

The boldness of him—so unapologetically devious

—makes something fierce bloom in my chest. His cock presses into my palm, and as much as I shouldn't, I clasp him, take the opportunity to tease him. I'm getting wet just thinking about us in the bathroom, what we could get up to. He's so big and rigid. I can't think straight, knowing how very clever he is with his appendage.

"I don't feel anything," I say, feigning ignorance.

He growls, the sound tipping the scales in his favor. I rarely deny him when he sounds so unhinged.

Before he says anything, he stands, raises one cocky brow, and then strides down the aisle toward the back of the plane. There is a bedroom back there, along with two bathrooms. Still, I can't follow him. Everyone would suspect what we're up to.

Like they haven't done it...

The reflection doesn't make me any braver. Still, after a couple of minutes of debate, I unbuckle my belt and follow him. I try not to make eye contact with anyone on the plane, and I almost make it before Lucien catches my attention. My skin burns at his knowing grin, and I quicken my steps, wanting to be out of the main cabin before I die of shame.

Heat floods my face, but beneath the embarrassment is something else—defiance. After everything we survived, I refuse to live timidly.

He's waiting for me, leaning against the bathroom

door like he knows I'll come. I shake my head. "I can't believe I'm allowing you to talk me into this."

He reaches for me and picks me up. I gasp, wrap my legs about his waist, and thank the heavens I've worn a long, flowing skirt. He strides into the bathroom and slams the door with his foot. This bathroom isn't like the ones on regular airliners. This one is opulent, large, and has a shower.

Marble countertops gleam beneath soft lighting. A full mirror spans one wall. There's enough space to move without bumping elbows—luxury designed for indulgence, not necessity. Even the air smells faintly of expensive cologne and leather.

"I can," he says, sitting me on the countertop. "You're a naughty girl."

The way he looks at me—like I'm his salvation and ruin all at once—makes my throat tighten. I never thought I'd find a love that feels this consuming and safe at the same time. I chuckle and devour the sight of him. His eyes darken with determination, and I reach for his t-shirt, ripping it from his body. I want to see him. All of him.

"Impatient." He kisses my nose, his fingers sliding my skirt out of the way before reaching for my panties. He slips them off and steps between my legs, his jeans coarse against my sensitive flesh. The contrast of rough denim and the cold mirror at my back makes every nerve ending spark. I get even wetter.

"Now that you've started this game, yes, I suppose I am," I say.

He licks his lips and then dips his head between my legs. With one long glide of his tongue, he licks me long and good. I buck against him, clasp his hair, and hold him where I ache most.

"Oh yes, Stephen." I bite my lip. "Just there. Right there." He works my clit with his tongue, slow, circular movements that send coils of desire to thrum through me. I want him so much. I'm so wet and needy that I undulate against his face with little inhibition.

The engine's vibration beneath us blends with the pulse between my thighs, and for a dizzy moment I feel suspended in more ways than one—between sky and sea, between need and ecstasy.

"You are so fucking sweet." He suckles my clit hard. "I love licking your sweet pussy."

I moan. I can feel my orgasm building fast. "Stephen, fuck me. Please. I want you to fuck me until I come."

He stands and rips his jeans open. I gasp as he thrusts hard and good. So damn good. I wrap my legs about his waist, pull him down for a kiss as he gives me what I want. Always satisfying me in all ways. "You feel so good." He fills me, and the intimacy—this claiming, this closeness—undoes me more than the pleasure alone ever could.

"So do you, baby."

I hold on to him, his large, rigid cock pressing all the right buttons as he thrusts into me. I call his name, oblivious of where we are or who we're with. I no longer care. I want him to fuck me until we both come. Lose ourselves in each other. "Fuck me. Hard."

He clasps my ass and pulls me close, the action making him deeper. I can't stop the tremors that steal my breath, my wits. He kisses me, his tongue tangling with mine, our mouths fused as my orgasm rips through me. It crashes with a force that feels emotional —release not just of pleasure but of strength, hard truths, the quiet rebuilding of a life we almost lost.

"Stephen," I gasp against his lips.

He swallows my cries with another kiss, and I moan as he fucks me, joining me in my release.

"God, I love you." His words are sweet, even when we're locked together as we now are, 30,000 feet in the air and having just fucked each other's brains out. There is a rawness in his voice that steals my breath more than the orgasm does. As if loving me is both his greatest strength and his deepest vulnerability.

"I love you too."

He meets my eyes, still inside me, refusing to let me go. "Marry me, Dallen. I love you so much, I don't ever want to lose you. Marry me, be my wife, my partner, the mother of our children. Be mine forever."

For a heartbeat, the world narrows to just us. My chest aches with the enormity of what he's asking—not because I doubt him, but because I know exactly what it means to choose him.

I clasp his jaw and meet his eyes. His solemn, vulnerable gaze. "What?" Possibly not the best answer, but this can't be real. This has to be a dream. A wonderful, beautiful dream.

He grins. "Marry me," he repeats.

I stare, unable to form words for a moment, but it is only for a figment of time. I'm not stupid. "Yes. Yes, I'll marry you." The word feels like stepping into sunlight after a year in the dark. Like choosing hope over fear. Like choosing him—every flawed, fierce, beautiful part of him—for the rest of my life.

He kisses me again, and just like that, I want him. He pulls back, smiling. "We should tell the others. Celebrate immediately."

And for the first time in a long time, the future doesn't terrify me. It thrills me.

"Lead the way..." *Fiancé...*

ALSO BY WILLOW YORK

VOWS OF BLOOD

King of Revenge

King of Fury

King of Deceit

ABOUT WILLOW YORK

Willow York isn't new to writing romance—but she's done playing nice. Now it's all about ruthless anti-heroes, forbidden desires, and steamy mafia drama that will leave you breathless and begging for more.

Made in the USA
Coppell, TX
02 March 2026

73054500R00138